"I am charmed by the book—text and pictures. It is no effort, of course, to be pleased by the sure touch—stories and animal drawings that are poetry, innate, humor-born, and wise."

—*Marianne Moore*

"Jaime de Angulo has drawn upon a fascinating collection of native California Indian folklore. Weaving fiction with fact, his first-hand knowledge of these tribes has enabled him to convey more of the authentic flavor than could have been possible in any literal translations."

—*Dr. Harry Tschopik,*
The American Museum of Natural History, New York

"One of the most outstanding writers that I have ever encountered."

—*William Carlos Williams*

INDIAN

Written and Illustrated by

with a foreword by

TALES

JAIME De ANGULO

CARL CARMER

BALLANTINE BOOKS • NEW YORK

Library of Congress Catalog Card Number: 52-11575

ISBN 0-345-25275-6-175

This edition published by arrangement with
Farrar, Straus and Giroux, Inc.

Manufactured in the United States of America

First Ballantine Books Edition: March, 1974
Second Printing: March, 1976

FOREWORD

Few men have the gift of transcending national origin and cultural heritage to enter intimately and understandingly into the life of a people alien to them by birth. Jaime de Angulo was such a man. His forty years of living among the Pit River Indians of California gave him the opportunity of identifying himself with his neighbors so completely and sympathetically that it might truly be said of him that no feeling was theirs which was not also his. His early years in his native Spain and his educational experiences at Johns Hopkins University in Maryland, while not so important to his final literary product, gave him the further advantages of perspective and objectivity without which this book could not be so important a contribution to our literature.

Jaime de Angulo had both the judgment and the intuition to realize that translation of atmosphere and feeling and fancy can not be left to scholars. Only over the bridge of his own creative imagination could he lead his readers across the barriers of a strange language and a distinctively different culture, into wise and true appreciation. He was a professed student of anthropology and in these pages some of his findings are recorded, but this book was written by a poet.

Other writers, Geoffrey Chaucer among them, have used the description of a fictional journey as a basic structure on which to stretch the colorful peltry of tale and poem which have charmed their readers. Had not Jamie de Angulo chosen to do likewise, much of the unity and quality which, taken together, make his story a work of art, would be lost. Had he not felt with many philosophers and critics before him that (in the words of George Moore) "Art begins in the irresponsible imaginings of the people" and decided that his vast knowledge of the religion, folk-ways, and distinctive characteristics of the Indians of the West should be the origin, inspiration, and background of his own original composition, these pages might have contained a prosaic report rather than a beautifully rhythmic and intensely poetic narrative.

The time of the action of this long narrative is that prehistoric dawn when men and animals were not so distinguishable from each other as they are today. The place is the Western plains and mountains of our North American continent. The animal-humans who lived there, the reader will discover, are at once recognizable as possessed of those unique traits which distinguish similar animals and humans today. The resultant world is a triumph of a poet's fancy, one in which he may indulge his knowledge of the past, his feeling for the present, his intuitive prophesies of the future. It is fundamentally a human world, and his knowledge of humans is deep. Through all of it, nevertheless, he is sensitively aware of the ethnic strain that provides the overtones. It is also an *American Indian* world and no writer of a language other than Indian has understood it so well. Here is all the ingenuous wonder, the experienced wisdom, the rollicking humor of the Indian presented with a sureness and clarity seldom if ever achieved. From the moment at the end of the first day's journey when, his family ready for bed on their rabbit-skin blankets, Bear speaks his goodnight prayer, the reader lives in an Indian world: "Good night, Mountains, you must protect us tonight. We are strangers but we are good people. We don't mean harm to anybody. Good night, Mister Pine Tree. We are camping under you. You must protect us tonight. Good night, Mister Owl. I guess this is your home where we are camped. We are good people, we are not looking for trouble, we are just traveling. Good night, Chief Rattlesnake. Good night, everyone. Good night, Grass People, we have spread our bed right on top of you. Good night, Ground, we are lying right on your face. You must take care of us, we want to live a long time."

Jaime de Angulo has packed his book with Indian folklore—with tall tales and jokes, ceremonial rituals and poetic allegories, blessings and curses, gambling games and hunting adventures. It is decorated with descriptions of the great plains and the high mountains of our West. These are things that will be valued by Americans of all ages. Children will be fascinated by the stories, amused by the humor, delighted by the rhythms of his words. Besides, with all of its subtle, beneath-the-surface meanings this is a simple book which may be enjoyed at face-value. To the older and more sophisticated reader it offers such rewards as only many readings will discover. They will read much even in his simplest verses:

> *A dragon fly came to me*
> *With news from my home.*
> *I lie in the afternoon,*
> *Looking toward the hills.*

As for those who thought that when Jaime de Angulo leaned over the water the last time before his untimely death, the whirligig bug stole his shadow, they are wrong. It will grow longer and longer over the land and the people he loved.

CARL CARMER

INDIAN TALES

AUTHOR'S PREFACE

You will ask a lot of questions, about Indian houses, and what is a center-post, and why is there a smoke-hole and no chimney? And how can you go in and out of the house by the smoke-hole without getting burned?

Well . . . in the first place, the fire is a small fire, just about the size of the camp-fire you build in the country when you are on a picnic. The Indian house is a pretty large affair. There is no chimney, but there is a large hole in the roof. That hole is part of the structure when you build the house. It is something like a hatchway on the deck of a ship. It is the main door of the house, as well as the way out for the smoke. At that height, the little bit of smoke and the heat from the fire are not enough to bother anyone going up or down the ladder. Anyway, the fire was always a small one. A big fire would make the house unbearably hot, since it was like a sort of cellar or cavern dug into the ground, and covered over with earth.

In making an Indian house, the first thing was to dig the ground. Everybody got together (a house like that was a kind of communal hall, and held from twenty to fifty, and even sixty people, sometimes) and dug into the ground with digging-sticks, scooped the earth into baskets with their hands, and piled it outside like a rim or round wall. The site of the house was always chosen on a knoll, for good drainage.

The next thing was to erect the center-post. That was the main thing. The center-post was a tree, some-

1

times as large around as a fat man, with a fork three or four times a man's height. It had to be felled in the woods (which was a long process, since the Indians had no metals, no axes—they worried the wood of the trunk with chisels made out of elk antlers and rocks for hammers; after a day or two, the shreds of wood would be dry enough to burn, then you started to worry the next two or three inches of wood around the trunk; it was a slow business, but the Indians were patient).

When the center-post was ready, it had to be dragged to the site of the house, everybody pulling, and then set up. That's when everybody quarreled and all those who thought they were chiefs gave advice, and the old fellows who really were chiefs and leaders kept silent and waited to say the last word.

Then you dragged the main rafter, or ridge-pole, which was a long, straight pine tree. The butt was laid on the rim of the house site, and the other end lifted, raised, and laid to rest into the fork of the center-post. And that took more shouting and quarreling.

Then you laid the secondary rafters, with one end resting on the ridge-pole, and the other end more or less radiating and resting on the rim. After that came a lot of small, short poles, like the ceilings in our frame houses. Then more branches and twigs. On top of that, large slabs of pine bark. Then, on top of it all, a layer of earth.

From the outside, at a distance, the whole thing was hardly visible. It was just a large mound of earth with grass growing over it; except that you might notice a plume of smoke coming out of it, and the ladder sticking out. You walked to the top, and peered down the hatchway, and it was like looking down into a cavern. You saw the fire, and then you could make out the shapes of people sitting around against the wall, or sprawling in the straw, or walking about, stepping over people lying down.

The aeration was fairly good, because there was a sort of tunnel running out. That provided a draft; the

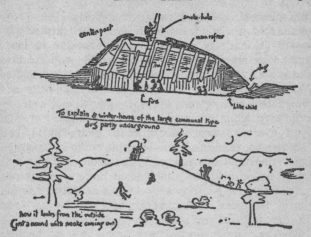

To explain a winter-house of the large communal type dug partly underground

how it looks from the outside
(just a mound with smoke coming out)

outside air was sucked in down through that tunnel and went out through the smoke-hole. And the dogs, and the little children big enough to crawl, but not big enough to climb the ladder, also used that runway or tunnel.

That was the old-time Indian house. It would last for ten or twenty years, until the timbers rotted. There may be a few of them yet, or their remains. But they are seldom built nowadays. Everywhere, the Indians have taken to living in shacks and dilapidated frame cabins. But every once in a while a small community of Indians living on a "ranchería" will get together and put up an old-time communal house for their dances and ceremonies of spring and autumn, at the time of the equinoxes. I myself helped build such a house (although of a slightly different type, with four center-posts and a door) at a ranchería near Ione, not so very far from San Francisco, some fifteen years ago.

I am speaking, of course, about the California Indians. They are the ones I know best. I went among them primarily as a professional linguist, to study their languages and dialects; also as a sort of amateur anthropologist, and perhaps general philosopher. I was interested in their ways of thinking, their attitude toward life and the spirit of religious wonder. I knew that they represented an extremely primitive stage of society. I went there armed with the usual arsenal of scientific theories I had culled out of textbooks and treatises. I soon learned to throw away all that baggage, and stop filling notebooks (except in linguistics), and just live with them—acorn soup, pinole mush, bad smells, smoke, dirt and all—and the eternal gossip, and bickering, and quarreling of the medicine men. It is not very hard to make the Indians accept you as one of themselves. As soon as you listen and don't ask too many (to them) fool questions, and especially as soon as they feel that you are sincere in not looking down on them as inferior brutes, they accept you as another human being.

Then you discover a lot of very interesting things about primitive thinking. Living among them, sprawling under the oak trees, watching the clouds or a procession of ants, or a hawk perching on a dead pine, you gossip, you talk about so-and-so and what a liar he is, or two old men start arguing about who made the world, and a young fellow tries to reconcile his knowledge of motors and the electric spark with Indian ideas of medicine and religion. Pretty soon you find yourself drifting into their lingo, and even their ways of thinking. Then you catch yourself with a start; you remember you are a white man, and supposed to be a scientist; and you wonder whether you are playing a game with yourself. You try to explain thought to yourself. You feel puzzled. You wonder whether you are dropping back into childhood and the wonder-time of stories, and fairies, and miracles, and marvelous things. And then you listen to another story of when the animals were men. . . .

I wrote these stories several years ago, for my children, when they were little. Some of them I invented out of my own head. Some of them I remembered—at least, parts, which I wove in and out. Some parts I actually translated almost word for word from my texts. I have not paid very much attention to scientific accuracy. I have mixed tribes that don't belong together. I have made some people live in a type of house that belonged to a different section of the country (there were many different types of construction, and many different types of social organization, and many other differences). So don't worry about it. If you find yourself getting interested in the subject, go to the literature. There is an excellent, comprehensive book on the Indians of California by Kroeber of the University of California. It was published in 1926 by the Smithsonian Institution, as Bulletin 78 of the Bureau of American Ethnology. It is a fat book; and you may find it pretty dry (but all the scientific books written by anthropologists are bound to be dry). But Kroeber knows the California Indians as nobody else does. And in his book you will find a complete bibliography.

I also have written a dozen or so articles. But they are mostly technical works on linguistics, and would put you to sleep in five minutes. One or two you might find interesting. There is one in French: "La Psychologie religieuse d'une tribu primitive,"[1] in which I discussed the religious feeling in a primitive tribe. This would be pretty difficult to obtain, except in the library of a university. It would be easier to get another article covering somewhat the same ground in a more succinct way: "The Background of the Religious Feeling in a Primitive Tribe."[2] Also "A New Religious Movement in North-Central California."[3]

If you are interested in folklore, you will find a translation I made of the creation myth of the Pomo

---

[1]"La Psychologie Religieuse des Achumawi," *Anthropos*, 1929, pp. 141-166, 561-589.

[2]*American Anthropologist*, Vol. 28, No. 2, April-June, 1926.

[3]*American Anthropologist*, Vol. 31, No. 2, April-June, 1929.

Indians.[4] Also "Miwok and Pomo Myths," in *Journal of American Folklore,* circa 1935. I published some interesting tales of a very different tribe, the Karok of northwestern California, in *International Journal of American Linguistics,* Vol. VI, Nos. 3 & 4, April, 1931. And, before I forget, two exceedingly striking tales from the Pit River tribe, in "Two Achumawi Tales," *Journal of American Folklore,* Vol. 44, April-June, 1931. That will hold you for a while. Once you get interested in these primitive Indians of California you will read more and more about them. It's too bad that most of the literature is of a technical nature, published in scientific journals. On the other hand, good, readable, interesting accounts or tales, such as are sometimes found in ordinary magazines, are usually not only inaccurate, but give a false idea of the Indian background. What they give you is the orthodox mixture of romantic and picturesque elements which is the usual conception of the Indian by the average white man. I may yet give a picture of the Indians in overalls, as I saw them, but I have first to find a publisher.[5]

Now, go ahead and read these tales of Father Bear, and Mother Antelope, and the little boy Fox. When you find yourself searching for some mechanical explanation, if you don't know the answer, invent one. When you pick out some inconsistency or marvelous improbability, satisfy your curiosity like the old Indian folk: "Well, that's the way they tell that story. I didn't make it up myself!"

JAIME DE ANGULO

[4]*Anthropos,* Tome XXVII, 1932. (If that is too difficult to get at there is another, with full Indian text, in *Journal of American Folklore,* Vol. 48, July-September, 1935.)

[5]PUBLISHER'S NOTE: See Appendix for excerpts from Mr. De Angulo's "Indians in Overalls," published in *The Hudson Review,* Autumn, 1950.

Come on, get ready, we are going to start this morning," said Bear coming back into the house. He was talking to his wife, Antelope. "The sun is shining; I don't think it will rain any more for a while. We must go and visit your sister who is living with the Crane people, and it's a long way from here. Come on, gather up your things, strap the baby on the cradle-board, pack enough food for a few days—jerked meat and dried fish and acorn meal—enough for several days on the trail. It's a long way from here to the village of the Cranes. Come on, Fox Boy, get ready. Let's get started."

Antelope strapped the baby Quail on the cradle-board, then she called to the little boy Fox, "Hurry up, put on your new moccasins." But the little boy Fox cried, "I don't want to put on my moccasins. I don't want to. I DON'T WANT TO!"

"Why don't you want to put on your moccasins? You can't travel barefoot. Nobody can. Feet get sore traveling all day."

"I don't want to. I DON'T WANT TO!"

"Don't you want to come and see the world?"

"Nooo, I don't want to, I don't want to!" cried the little boy Fox, stamping his foot.

"Oh, I see," said Bear. "You've got the HA-HAS this morning. That's too bad, that's too bad. Well, all right, you'd better stay here, then, and watch the house for us until we return. Come on, Antelope, let's go."

7

So they started along the trail. Bear was packing the
food on his back and in his hand he held his bow and
the arrows were in the quiver on his back. Antelope
carried on her back the baby Quail strapped on the
cradle-board, and in her hand she held her digging-
stick.

They started along the trail, *tras . . . tras . . . tras,*
and pretty soon the little Fox came running after them
with his moccasins in his hand.

"Wait for me, wait for me. I want to see the world!"
So they waited for him to sit down and put on his new
moccasins.

"Why, you've got them on the wrong foot, little boy!
The other way, the other way."

"Why, you've got them on the wrong foot, little
boy! The other way, the other way."

Now they started again along the trail, but Fox cried,

"Oh, I forgot my bow-and-arrows. I have to have my bow-and-arrows to hunt."

"All right, hurry up. We'll wait for you."

He came back crying, "I can't find them, I can't find them!" The little Fox Boy was standing in the middle of the trail, crying and rubbing the tears with his tail.

"Oh, I see," said Bear, "you've got the HA-HAS again. That's bad. You'll never be a man, I'm afraid. You'll never be a hunter. It never was that a hunter cried because he couldn't find his bow-and-arrows. Hunters always put their things away carefully. But we'll help you find them this time. Maybe you'll learn. Maybe you'll be a man some day."

And now they started on the trail again, *tras . . .*

tras . . . tras. They stopped at the house of Turtle Old Man, he was Bear's uncle; they stopped in front of his house and called. He heard them and he stuck his head out of the smoke-hole. There was no door to his house and no window, just a hole in the roof for the smoke from the fire to go out. And the smoke-hole was for a door also. He stuck his head out and called, "Hey! What do you want? Where are you all going?"

"We are going west, we are on our way to visit our relatives who live near the ocean." And Fox Boy added, "I am going to play with my cousins."

"Wait a minute," said Turtle Old Man. "I'll give you some beads to take as a present. It never was that you go and visit people without bringing them some little thing. And when you get to the Hawks' village, give these arrowheads to the two Hawk Chiefs and tell them to send me some good flint from their Mountain of Black Glass. And don't forget to stop at Coyote's house. Coyote Old Man is a fine doctor, a great medicine man. And here is a cocoon rattle for him. I've made it very carefully. But don't stop at Weasel's house. He is a bad man, he burned the world once because he was mad. You'd better leave him alone, he doesn't like people. Well, good-by. I'll watch over your house while you are gone."

And now they started on the trail again, *tras . . . tras . . . tras.* They traveled all day and in the evening they got to the top of a ridge from which they could see the ocean, far away. Not far from there they found a spring of water under some big pine trees.

"Here is a good place to camp," said Bear. "Gather some fire-wood while I go hunt a rabbit."

"No, let me hunt the rabbit," said Fox, and he went out with his bow-and-arrows, but very soon he came back crying, "The rabbits won't keep still."

Antelope said, "You go after them too fast. You must learn to creep up to them slowly. It takes a long time to learn to be a hunter; it takes a long time to learn to be a man or a woman."

"Well, what shall I do?" asked the little Fox, sucking the end of his tail.

"Take your tail out of your mouth and go and get some fire-wood."

"No, I don't want to. It's too heavy. I don't want to. No, no, NO!" Little Fox got into a rage and started to stamp his foot, and he got so mad that he stamped on his own tail!

"Listen, I'll go and gather fire-wood. You swing your sister Quail and keep her quiet. That's a good job for an older brother."

"Oh, yes, I can do that," said Fox. Antelope hung the cradle-board from a pine branch and went after fire-wood.

Now Bear came back with two cottontail rabbits. They roasted them on the coals of the fire and ate them with acorn bread, then they spread their rabbit-skin blankets on the ground.

Then Bear called, "Good night, Mountains, you must protect us tonight. We are strangers but we are good people. We don't mean harm to anybody. Good night, Mister Pine Tree. We are camping under you. You must protect us tonight. Good night, Mister Owl. I guess this is your home where we are camped. We are good people, we are not looking for trouble, we are just traveling. Good night, Chief Rattlesnake. Good night, everyone. Good night, Grass People, we have spread our bed right on top of you. Good night, Ground, we are lying right on your face. You must take care of us, we want to live a long time."

Fox was sleeping between his parents, and between him and Antelope there was the little baby Quail. Fox said, "Oh, look! The sun is coming back on the other side!"

"No, little boy, that's the moon. He is the elder brother of the sun and he works at night."

"Oooh! Well, good morning, Mister Moon."

"No, silly, you mean good night."

"No, I don't. It's good morning for the moon."

"All right. Go to sleep." Bear was already snoring.

And now Antelope sat up. She looked into the shadows and sang softly a song to the night. It said: "Dream for my child so that he will have power."

The next morning Bear woke up early, long before the sun was up. It was the very beginning of the break of dawn when Bear sat up and started to sing. He was singing softly to himself, sort of humming. Then he got up and stretched himself and went to the spring to wash his face. He started a campfire while it was yet all dark. Then he started to cook breakfast. He was heating stones, small round stones.

"Mother, what was he singing? Who is that man he said was coming over the mountains from the east singing with the daylight?"

"Oh, he was singing about his shadow. That song is what the shadow sings. Your shadow, also. You must make him sing that way in the morning. Everybody's shadow comes home in the dawn, singing like that."

"But what do you mean, 'comes home'?"

"Sure, he comes home to you, your shadow does. You are his home."

"But where has he been?"

"Oh, he's been going around during the night, visiting, going places, and in the morning he comes home to you."

"Does he always come?"

"No, sometimes he gets lost. That's why your father was singing. We are in a strange place; his shadow might be wandering around, looking for him. But if the shadow hears him singing, he says to himself, 'Oh, that's me over there. That's where I belong.' "

"And if he gets lost, what happens then?"

13

"Then you get sick and you die. You can't keep on living without your shadow."

Fox Boy thought a moment, then he said, "But Father is not going to die because he's singing and his shadow must have heard him. I'd better sing too, so my shadow will hear me."

"Do you think you can remember the song? Listen, we'll sing it together.

'I'm coming, I'm coming. Over the mountains I come home.
I'm coming, I'm coming. With the daylight I come home.
I'm coming, I'm coming. From the east I come home.

Now, look, we'd better get up and help Bear cook breakfast."

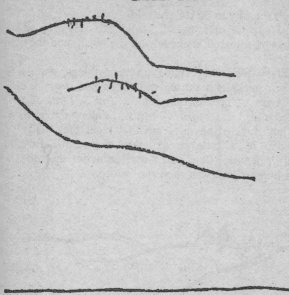

So they got up and washed their faces at the spring. Then Antelope took some acorn flour and made a mush. Then she picked some hot stones from the fire with a couple of sticks and dropped them into the mush which was in a small basket. The hot stones made a hissing sound, *hwishshshshhh, hwishshshshsh, hwish*. Pretty soon the mush was bubbling and boiling. Little Fox Boy couldn't wait. He put his two finger in the mush.

"Ouch!" he yelled, jumping up and down and shaking his fingers.

"Well, why don't you wait and let it cool a little? Nobody is going to take it away from you. Take your time, take your time. It never was that people couldn't wait a minute. Watch me. Watch how I do it."

Now Antelope deftly scooped some mush with her two fingers and she licked them off, quickly, just like that!

"That's the way to do it," she said.

"Oh, I can do that, myself," said Fox. He was so quick·that he smeared his nose with the mush, and they all laughed.

Breakfast over, they rolled up their things, shouldered their packs and started traveling again, *tras . . . tras . . . tras . . .* up the trail, *tras . . . tras . . . tras . . .* down the trail, *tras . . . tras . . . tras . . .* along the level trail. They traveled all day, and that night they made their camp by a little stream. And Fox Little Boy crawled in between Bear and Antelope under the rabbit-skin blanket and was soon fast asleep.

The next afternoon they reached the village of the Hawks.

"Where is the house of the Chief?"

"Over there. Right there, that's their house. The two Hawk Chiefs, Big Blue Hawk and Little Sparrow Hawk. They are the chiefs of this place."

"That house over there?"

"Yes, that's the house."

"Hawk Chief! Hawk Chief!"

"Well, whadyouwant? Whydyou make so much noise? The door is on the east side."

"Don't speak that way," said Blue Hawk to Sparrow Hawk. "You are too rough. Haven't you got any manners? Howdyou know but that these people are important people come to visit us! And you treat them rough like that. . . . Come in, come in. Go around. You people aren't used to our country. We don't come in and go out through the smoke-hole here; we have a door. Go right around to the east side. Come right in."

But the Sparrow Hawk had already flown out. He went out through his own door. He had a hole in the side of the wall by the side of the big door, a door all for himself, just his size. He went out, he was mad. He flew out into the night.

"Come right in," said Blue Hawk. They went in,

Bear and Antelope stooping under the lintel in the doorway and Fox stooping also.

They all sat around the fire and Antelope was unpacking the baby Quail. All the Hawk people came in, one by one, and sat on their heels around the wall. Then Blue Hawk Chief spoke. "You are welcome here. You have come a long way; you are welcome."

"We didn't know where the door was."

"Our people have the door on the side. Maybe your people have the smoke-hole for a door. That's a good way, too."

"But somebody spoke about another door."

"Oh, that's my older brother, that's Sparrow Hawk. Don't pay any attention to him. He is a bad one, he is a mean one. That's his door there. . . . You see that little door there? Well, that's his door—can't come in through the main door like everybody else—must have HIS OWN little door. He never grew up. I don't know why. Some people say it's because he had the HA-HAS when he was a little boy. They say it keeps them from growing up properly. . . . I don't know. It's possible. I remember he used to cry and yowl and stamp his foot and say, 'I don't want to, I don't want to, I don't want to!' just like that. Seems that's the way they sing when they have got a bad case of HA-HAS. Anyway, he never grew up, stayed small and mean. But there he comes, I hear him. Listen." And out in the night they heard his song coming nearer and nearer.

Ya' ya henna ya' ya henna . . .

They all looked toward the small hole by the side of the main door. Sparrow Hawk flew in, making a zigzag and a loop, and then stood above their heads, flapping his wings. Then he alighted in the cleared space in front of the fire and said "Hello."

"Hello, yourself!" said Fox Boy, and he roared with laughter. "I want to play with that little boy. I like him!"

Everybody roared with laughter. Sparrow Hawk cried, "All right, I'll play with you. Come on."

"Watch out, boy, watch out. He is a hard one to handle. He is spoiled. But if you want to keep him for a pet, you can have him. We won't miss him."

The Fox Boy then grabbed the Sparrow Hawk. They had a lively tussle on the floor and almost rolled into the fire. Fox gave a yell and let the Hawk loose; the Hawk had bitten him on the thumb.

Fox cried, "I don't want him for a pet. You can keep him."

The Sparrow Hawk flew out through his own little door and they could hear his war song diminishing in the night.

Fox Boy was nursing his thumb. All the Hawk people were rocking with laughter. Blue Hawk was laughing too; he cried, "Let him go. You are not losing much of a pet. I sort of thought you couldn't handle him. He may be small but he is hard to handle."

Now the Hawk people were settling for the night, choosing places for themselves here and there around the wall of the house. Bear picked up his pack and started for the door.

"Where are you going?" asked the Blue Hawk Chief.

"I'm going out to look for a place for us to sleep."

"No, you don't need to do that. Sleep right here with us. Plenty of room. Make your bed here inside anywhere. I see you have a rabbit-skin blanket. How do you make those blankets?"

"Oh, it's easy," said Antelope. "It's not much of a trial. It only takes patience and a LOT of rabbits, about two hundred rabbits! Cut the skins into long strips, then twist them—that makes the fur stick out—then weave the strips together. That's all."

"Well, well," said Blue Hawk Chief, "you are clever people."

"And I helped my mother twist the strings," said Fox Boy proudly.

"Well, well, you did! And did you catch the rabbits too?"

"Nope," said Fox, "they won't keep still."

All the Hawks roared with laughter, and Fox Boy laughed with everybody.

And now they were settling themselves for the night. Blue Hawk Chief called, "Fire tender, fire tender, where are you? Poke the fire, put some twigs to burn and give us a light to make our beds."

When Bear left early the next morning, Hawk Chief said, "I ought to give you some obsidian flint as a present for your uncle, Turtle Old Man, but I haven't any left. But go by the village of the Flint people. They live right at the foot of Black Glass Mountain. That mountain is made entirely of black obsidian, and some of it is just right for knives and arrowheads. But the Flint people have the sole rights to it. You can get it only through them. They are crusty people, quick to anger, but it's only the surface. They really are good people if you don't get offended at first. Here is some venison; give it to them as a present from me."

Bear, Antelope, Fox, and baby Quail started on the trail. *Tras . . . tras . . . tras . . .* they traveled all day, *tras . . . tras . . . tras . . .* along the trail, and they arrived at last at the village of the Flint people at the foot of the Black Glass Mountain

"Where is the house of the Chief?"

"That's his house over there, the house of the two brothers who are Chiefs of this place. But you'd better not stop here. This is not a good place to stop. We are dangerous people, we are brittle, we are hard, we get mad easily."

"Ho, Chief! Ho, Chief!"

"Well, whadyou want? Come in here if you want to fight."

"No, no, we don't want to fight. We didn't come here to fight, we came here to visit you and bring you a present from Hawk Chief, a nice piece of deer liver."

The younger Flint took it; he sliced it against his nose into thin slices and threw them to his dog.

"I don't like liver," he said. "Give me some good tough meat from the neck to chew."

Antelope fished into her pack, she took out some dried jerky and offered it to the Flints. The elder Flint took it, he stamped on it and cut it into little pieces for his dog.

"I don't like soft meat," he said. "I always eat a young Fox for supper." But Fox Boy strutted up to him.

"You'd better not eat me, I warn you. I might poison you because I've got the HA-HAS!!!"

"Ho, ho, ho," laughed the elder Flint, "he is a poison man, he's a medicine man, he's a powerful one!"

The younger Flint said, "Better leave him alone, brother. Better not challenge him. Maybe he is a good gambler—he might beat you." The Flints were laughing so hard they were crying.

All the Flint people had been coming into the house of the Chiefs and now they were sitting themselves around the wall. In bending their knees and elbows they made squeaky sounds, and when two of them jostled each other, they clinked. Indeed, they were strange to look at with their long thin bodies of dark obsidian glass; they were so thin that you could hardly see them from the front, and from the side you could see through them as through smoked glass. In fact, these Flint people were very sharp on their edges.

They were laughing and egging on their chief.

"Go on, challenge that boy to a hand game. Maybe he is a good guesser; maybe he is a good gambler; maybe he's got power."

Fox Boy cried, "Maybe I haven't got much power yet because I am only a boy, but I'm not afraid to gamble with you if my father will play on my side. *He* is a good gambler and singer, he knows many gambling songs, he'll take you on."

"How about it, Mr. Bear?"

Bear laughed. "All right, I'll help my boy."

Now the two Flint Chiefs sat on each side of the fire and Bear and Fox sat on the ground on the other side of the fire. Then somebody gave Bear and Fox each a pair of gambling bones; they were made of the shin bones of deer. Bear looked at them.

"You people use pretty long bones. You can hardly hide them in your hands. You must be afraid of cheaters."

"Oh, cheating's all right as long as you don't get caught, but if you get caught, you lose the game right there and then. That's the rule with us."

"Yes, we also have the same rule. And which bone do you guess, the one tied with black string or the naked white one?"

"We guess the naked one."

"All right, we are all set."

"You are the visitors, you start hiding them."

Bear and Fox started their song.

Bo le em na, bolem bo lem . . .

The two Flint Chiefs were the guessers; they were studying the faces of Fox and Bear across the fire. One of the Flints nudged his brother.

"You guess."

"All right, brother . . . guess the middle . . . I think. . . ." Now he guessed; he shouted "HA!" with his arm straight out, palm vertical, which meant he guessed both naked bones in the middle. He guessed Bear right but he missed Fox. So Bear threw his bones across to the Flints, and the Flints paid one counter for the guess they had missed. And now Fox hid his bones again. This time the Flints guessed him right, and he threw his bones across, and it was now the turn of Bear and Fox to do the guessing.

"You shoot," Bear whispered to Fox. (Bear was a poor guesser, he could hide the bones all right but he was not a good shooter—he thought too long before making up his mind.) So he whispered to Fox, "You shoot them." But Fox Boy was bashful in front of strangers, so he whispered back, "You ask my mother." So Bear signaled to Antelope and she came and knelt by the side of Bear and Fox. Antelope was known at home as a good gambler, especially a good shooter. And now she studied the faces of the Flints. She looked at them hard in the dim light of the fire. Finally, she made them nervous and before she had time to call "HA!" they changed their song so as to throw her off. But they couldn't fool Antelope; she shouted "HA!" and got them both. Everybody laughed; the Flints threw their bones across, and Bear and Antelope took them up. Bear whispered to her, "Let's fool them, wife. Let's sing that song we learned from that eastern man. I'm sure they've never heard it." So they did. Now the Flints shot; they got Bear but they missed Antelope; they missed her again and again. At home she had the reputation of being one of the best gamblers.

And so it went for a long time—sometimes the Flints won, and sometimes Bear and Antelope won. Little

Fox Boy got sleepy and sneaked off to bed. The Flints made room for him and spread a blanket over him. The game went on for a while, then Antelope said, "You must excuse us, but it's getting late. We are traveling people, we are on a long journey to visit our relatives near the coast, over the mountains."

"That's right, that's right," said the Flint Chief. "We had all better go to bed. Fire tender, fire tender! throw some twigs on the fire. Make a blaze, so we can see where we make our beds. Where is that little boy? Oh, oh, oh, he is already asleep. Fine boy, fine boy. He is, a good gambler already. Good night, everyone."

In the morning when they were getting ready to go, the Flint Chief, who had taken a great liking to Fox, gave him a little buckskin sack to hang from his belt. In the sack were a handful of arrowheads made of obsidian flint; beautiful arrowheads like smoked glass, well-chipped on both sides, and the edges straight to a point.

"Here, boy, take this as a present from the Flint tribe. These flints will be your luck, your *dinihowi*. If you should get into trouble, take them out of the little sack, shake them in your hand, and then listen to what they say. They will help you. But don't go near Weasel's house. He is a bad one. He burned the world once, long ago. Well, good-by, Mrs. Antelope, Mr. Bear. Good-by, little baby Quail. Have a good journey. We'll play hand games again when you come back this way."

So now Antelope shouldered the cradle-board and Bear shouldered the pack of provisions. His bow was in his hand and the arrows were in the quiver on his back. Fox Boy also carried his bow-and-arrows and hanging from his belt the little buckskin sack with the flints in it.

Tras . . . tras . . . tras . . . up the trail, *tras . . . tras . . . tras . . .* down the trail, *tras . . . tras . . . tras . . .* along the level trail, all morning they traveled until they came to a stream. Bear went across first to test the depth—the water reached only to his knees—then Antelope went across and they called back to Fox to

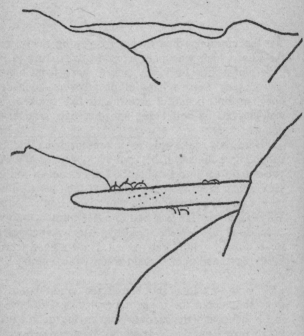

take off his moccasins and hurry up. But just then he had a fit of HA-HAS. He was jumping up and down and stamping his foot.

"I don't want to! I don't want to! I don't want to!" he yelled.

It was a *very* bad fit of HA-HAS indeed.

"All right," they cried, "just stay there, then. We're going on."

When they disappeared beyond the ridge, Fox dashed across the river. He rushed along the trail as fast as he could—he never even stopped to examine the

tracks. Very soon he lost the trail . . . then he found it again, but maybe it was another trail. Then he went back a little way, then he lost the trail again. *Now* he was completely, utterly lost. He began to run and he ran and ran, just flying in front of his tail. He stopped out of breath on top of a ridge, with his heart pounding. He cried a little; he was whimpering, "I wish I could get cured of having HA-HAS." Then he remembered the flints in their sack. He took them out, he shook them in his hands and put them to his ear.

"Oh, my little flints, help me. Where are we?"

The flints said, "We can't see from here. Send one of us up in the air."

"How can I do that?"

"Easy. Tie one of us to the end of an arrow."

Fox Boy took one of the flints; he tied it to the end

of an arrow; he strung it in his bow, he drew the bow-string back, he aimed the arrow straight up and shot. The arrow went up, up, up, and came down.

"Did you see them, my flint?"

"Yes, they are not far away. I saw them going over a hill over there to the west, but you'd better hurry because the sun is getting low and I saw a hunter coming back beyond a hill. It must be Weasel."

Fox Boy picked up his bow-and-arrows and he lit down the slope, he laid out his tail; uphill and downhill he ran.

"Wait for me! Wait for me!"

"We always have to wait for you while you have your HA-HAS. It never was that people traveling had to wait for someone with the HA-HAS. We won't wait for you any more."

Antelope was already making camp. They made a fire. They ate, they spread their beds on the ground. Bear said good night to all the people of the place, the trees, and the grass, and the ground, and the bird people who live in the tops of the trees, and all the crickets, and all the people who travel around in the nighttime. Fox crawled into bed between his parents.

In the morning Antelope said, "You'd better sing for your shadow. He'll need it to find you in this fog." The fog was so thick that they could hardly see Bear ten paces away where he was building the fire. He was shivering and grumbling to himself.

Fox said, "Where are we going today?"

Bear answered, "How do I know? How do you expect me to know where anyone is going in this fog!"

"Oh, oh, oh, Father has got the HA-HAS this morning! Maybe I should ask my flints." Little Fox shook his bag of flints.

Fog in the east,
Fog in the north,
Fog in the west,
Fog in the south,
A good flint always goes straight.

That's what the flints were singing inside their sack.

"What do they mean, Father?"

"I don't know. Ask your mother."

"Shoot a flint, boy. Shoot an arrow."

"But I've lost my bow." Little Fox began to cry.

"You shouldn't have laid it on the ground so carelessly. But never mind now, you can't find it in this fog. Take your father's bow. I'll help you pull it. And don't cry, little boy. One day when your father is in a good humor, we'll ask him to make you a spear. It takes a long time to make a bow."

When he heard the arrow whizz by him, Bear jumped and nearly fell into the fire, but he didn't say anything, he merely took notice of the direction of the arrow and made a mark on the ground.

Now they finish their breakfast. Now they pack up. Now they start in the direction of the arrow, *tras . . . tras . . . tras . . .* up the trail, *tras . . . tras . . . tras . . .* down the trail, *tras . . . tras . . . tras . . .* walking along in the morning, Bear with his pack, Antelope with the baby Quail in her cradle-board, Fox Boy with the spear that his father had made for him.

"Why did we leave so early?"

"Because we have a long way to go."

"Are we going to Coyote's village?"

"Coyote has no village. Coyote is an old man. He lives all alone."

"Mother, are we going west?"

"We are going west, we are going west. Keep along."

"Father, are we going west?"

"We are going west, we are going west. Keep along."

"But, Sister, you little one, are we going west?" She didn't answer; she was laughing in her pack.

Old Coyote was sleeping in the hills.
Old Coyote was sleeping in his house.
His house was back in the back of the hills
In a little valley, in a hidden valley away back in
the hills.

They tramped all day along the trail; they went over
a ridge and down into a valley and over another ridge
and down again and around small hills. They found a
spring and a nice camping place and there they
camped that night. Bear said good night to all the trees
of the place, to the ground, to the grass, to the people
who move in the night.

Early in the morning they went along the trail again,
down the trail, winding in and out of the valleys in the
hills. They didn't pass any villages. There were no villages, no people. They wound in and out of the valleys
between the hills; the silent valley; the trail winding in
and out through the brush, through the chaparral. Just
about noontime, they came to a house.

"Grandfather! Grandfather!"
Nobody answered.
"Grandfather, Grandfather, where is the door?"
Nobody answered.

"Grandfather, oh! Grandfather, we're bringing you beads, nice, even, well-polished beads, four sacks of them."

Old Man Coyote stretched himself and yawned.

"There is no door to my house. I don't know how you're going to get in."

"I know how to get in," said Fox Boy. "Through the smoke-hole."

"No, no, you'd better not do that," grumbled Coyote from inside the house. "There is no center-post to my house, and no ladder, and you might drop into the fire. I don't know how you are going to get in. You'd better keep traveling. Go to some other place. Nobody's been here for a long, long time. I've been asleep and now you come and wake me up. I tell you, you can't get into this house because there is no door. I don't know how you are going to get in!!!"

"Grandfather, we are coming down, we are coming down through the smoke-hole. The flints are carrying us down."

"Oooooh," said Coyote, "that's different. You've got the flints with you, eh? All right, come down, come down. I guess I can't help it. I guess I had better wake up. Come on in. Come down, come down." So they came down the smoke-hole.

"I am an old man. There is nobody to help me. There is not much food in the house. My grandsons went away a long time ago. Maybe you've met them; Hawk Chiefs they are. They've got a village somewhere back in the hills. Maybe you came through their place. I guess they gave you those flints the little boy is carrying in the bag hanging from his belt. That's fine, good boy, medicine boy. What's your name?"

"I am Fox."

"Oooh, so you are Fox Little Boy. You must be the one."

"I don't know. I am Fox."

"Are you the Little Fox Boy who has the HA-HAS so often?"

"Nooo, I am Fox all right, and I guess I am a little boy yet, and I had a slight case of HA-HAS a long time ago, but *I am cured now* and I came with my parents to see the world. Are you Coyote Old Man?"

"Yees . . . I *think* I am Coyote Old Man. And you? You must be a big medicine man. You must be full of power. I guess you have come to gamble with me."

"Grandfather, grandfather, don't pay any attention to him. He is only a Fox Little Boy," Bear said. "He hasn't learned to gamble yet. You might hurt him."

"What about you, then? You are a big man. You must be a good gambler?"

"No, no, grandfather, we haven't come here to gamble. You might hurt us."

"Well, then, why have you come to my house?"

"We came to tell you that Turtle Old Man is still alive. He told us to come and tell you."

"Ho, Ho! That's good, that's good. I'm glad to hear that. The old man is still alive! Well, well, I'm glad to hear that. I'm glad you came and told me. You must have come a long way. You must be tired. It's hard to get here. I guess you never could have found the way without the help of that little boy. Maybe he'll be a medicine man some day."

"No, no, grandfather, I don't think he will ever be a medicine man."

"Nooo? Well, maybe he'll be a hunter?"

"No, no, grandfather," said Bear, "I don't think so. He gets the HA-HAS too often for that."

"Well, maybe he'll be a war man, a care-for-nothing man, a crazy man who is never afraid."

"I DON'T KNOW WHAT I WILL BE," said Fox. "I'll tell you when I am grown up. But I'll tell you what you might be telling me, and that's a good old-time story! Turtle Old Man said you knew a lot of old-time stories, real old-time stories. *That's* what I came here for!"

"So you want an old-time story," said Coyote Old Man. "All right, I'll tell you how Weasel burned the world."

. . . . They were living at Tuleyomi, Coyote Old Man, his wife, who was Pelican Queen, and his two grandsons, the Big Blue Hawk, Wekwek Hoypu, and his elder brother, Wiwwa Wekwek, the little Sparrow Hawk. Those two were Chiefs.

Well, one day Hawk Chief went hunting ducks, and while he was hunting he saw Weasel's house on a hillside. He went there, he went into the house, but there was no one in the house. Then he found some acorn mush and he ate it and a bit of squirrel that he found in the ashes of the fire. Then he went looking around and he found some beads, four sacks of them, four sacks full of beads. Hawk Chief took them; he went to the creek and hid them in the water, then he got scared and he ran home and he went to bed without eating his supper.

When Weasel came home and went into his house, he knew right away that someone had been there. He went over to the place where he kept his beads . . . the place was empty! *The beads were gone!* The beads were gone! The beads were gone. Then he got mad, *then he got mad,* he got madDER AND MADDER AND FOR FOUR DAYS he cried. Then he stopped crying and he went outside with his eyes swollen and he looked around. Then, they say, he made a fire. He made a fire, a hot fire, by blowing on it, and stuck his spear into it. The fire made the spear hot, red-hot. Then Weasel sang his war song. He danced, he stomped around the fire, singing,

Ya' ya henna, ya . . .

He was singing, "You want to try me, eh? You are not afraid of me? All right, I'll find you, wherever you are."

Then Weasel pulled his spear out of the fire and pointed it to the east. He pointed it to the north, he pointed it to the west. He pointed it to the south and there he found Hawk Chief, away down south over the mountains where he lived with Coyote Old Man and Pelican Queen.

They were all sitting around the fire when Hawk saw that spear coming out of the fire at him.

"Give him back his beads! Give him back his beads!"

"I stole them. I had them in the creek," the Hawk Chief was crying, running around the center-post.

"What's the matter with you?" asked Coyote Old Man.

Then, they say, the world caught fire . . . the whole world caught fire. It was burning, burning everywhere, up the canyons and down the slopes and over the flats. For days and nights it burned.

At last Coyote Old Man thought, "I ought to stop that

fire. Where's my rain sack?" He went to the hiding place under the eaves and took out his rain sack, then he went out to a redwood tree and beat the sack against the tree.

Fog, fog, fog,
Foggy rain, foggy rain,
Drop . . . drip . . . drip . . . drip. . . drip, drip, drip,
drip.

Old Man Coyote went back into the house and took up the elk horn in which he had been boring a hole.

"Grandfather, what are you doing?"

"Oh, nothing. Just having a little something to eat."

Rain, rain, rain, ten days and ten nights it rained. The world ceased burning. It rained and rained and kept on raining. Water was rushing down the creeks; in the bottoms of the valleys the water was rising like a lake. The water was rising around the house; it rose to the roof, it started to pour in at the smoke-hole. Hawk Chief flew out of the house.

"We'e'e'ek, we'e'e'ek, tlan, tlan, tlan, tlan, we'e'ek," he went, circling over the world four times, looking for a place to land.

Even the top of the Old Mountain was just under the water, but on the very top there was a branch of a bush sticking out. Hawk Chief perched on it. He was so tired! But that branch kept bobbing up and down, it kept ducking the Hawk in and out of the water.

"Grandfather! Grandfather! Catch me! I am drowning!"

But Coyote Old Man couldn't hear; he was inside the hole in the elk horn and he was singing.

On top of the Old Mountain two Diving Duck old men were swimming about. Hawk saw them.

"Grandfathers! Grandfathers, catch me! Oh, Grandfathers, I am drowning. Grandfathers, Grandfathers, catch me!"

One of the two old Ducks came close.

"All right, drop on my back."

Hawk Chief dropped and the Old Man Duck plunged with him under the water, down to their house under the water. There they made a bed for him and there he lay for eight days.

Now, they say, the world was free of water. It went down, little by little, down the sides of the big mountains, and down the hillsides, but the bottoms of the valleys were still full of mud.

Then Coyote Old Man missed the Hawk Chief, his grandson. He missed him and he cried. He went around looking for him, crying.

Then the Diving Duck old men woke the Hawk in their house.

"Get up, get up, it's time for you to get up. You are all right now."

So Hawk got up and they gave him something to eat, and he ate, they say. Then he took out his beads; he made two strings of them and hung them about the necks of the two old men. They were pleased.

"Ho! ho! grandson, thank you, thank you!"

"Well, good-by, Grandfathers. I am going to look for Coyote Old Man."

"All right, good-by, but why do you want to look for that old rascal?"

So the Hawk went and still he went. He went all around looking for his grandfather. Everywhere the world was still full of mud and it was dark and it was cold. At last he arrived at Tuleyomi. He stood on one side of the creek, and on the other side there was a man standing.

"Who are you?" asked that man.

"And you, who are you?"

"First you tell me who *you* are."

"No, no, you tell me first what *your* name is."

"The world has been destroyed! Where are you going? You must be full of power to be still alive!"

"Well, you seem to be full of power, yourself," said Hawk Chief, and he added, "Come on, hurry up, tell me who you are before I kill you!"

"Very well then, I'll tell you who I am. I am Coyote Old Man!

"And I am Hawk Chief!"

"Grandson, Grandson, *huyey!*" Coyote cried. From the other side he jumped across the creek and threw his arms around his grandson. He put Hawk Chief on his shoulders and took him home to his house and he made a bed for him and there they stayed.

In those days the world was dark, there was no fire, and Hawk Chief didn't like it. He grumbled, "Why is there no fire and no sun? Grandfather, why don't we have fire?"

"Well, everything is destroyed, nothing left. You are

just a boy, you don't understand the destruction of the world."

"Oh, you could get them for us if you wanted to."

"How can I?"

"Oh, you could if you wanted to."

"All right, I'll go and look for the fire."

So Coyote Old Man started out the next morning. TON*no-no-nonononono* . . . he arrived at the house of the two Rat Brothers. He called, "Hey, Grandsons, hey!"

One of the Rats answered from inside, "Well, the door is right there on the south side."

The other Rat scolded his brother.

"What's the matter with you? What are you mad about? That's no way to talk to a visitor. How do you know but it might be somebody of importance, a chief of some tribe? As a matter of fact, I see it's Grandfather Coyote. There must be something wrong for Grandfather to be traveling so far from his home. Come in, Grandfather. Come on in. You are welcome. And what brings you around this way?"

Old Man Coyote came in and sat down, then he opened the little buckskin sack hanging around his neck and pulled out a string of beads. He pulled out and pulled out a long string of beads. He cut the string and knotted the end beads and he gave the string to one Woodrat. Then he pulled out another string of beads and gave it to the other Woodrat.

"Your cousin wants fire. That's why I came," Coyote said. "I want you two to find it and bring it back for him. I know there are some people in the South World who still have fire but they keep close watch on it so nobody will steal it. I am too old to go, but you two are young and you are known as good runners."

"All right, all right, Grandfather, tomorrow we'll start. We'll stop by your house on our way. You can count on us."

Now Coyote Old Man went back home along the trail, TON*no-no-nonononono*. When he came to his house Hawk Chief asked, "Did you find those two, Grandfather?"

"Which two?"

"The two fire-stealers. Those two who are good for fire-stealing."

"How do you know about them?"

"But did you find them? Tell me, did you find them?"

"They said they would be here tomorrow."

The next morning the Woodrats arrived.

"Here we are," they said. "We told you we would come. We have been talking about it. It's pretty hard to steal fire from those people in the South World, even a spark of it. They don't let anyone take any of it. But we'll try to steal a little of it for you, for your grandson. It's pretty hard to live without fire."

"Good," said Coyote Old Man. He went to a corner of the house, he fumbled for a while under the rafters, and he came back with two pieces of punkwood. He gave one of these to the first Woodrat, and the other to the second Woodrat. The two of them set out on the run, the two fire-stealers, so the people say.

South World!
South World!
South World!
South World!

There is a gate there, *tututututututu.* As it opened of itself from the other side, they slipped through, the two fire-stealers, the Woodrats. It slammed together after them, and they went on, running abreast.

There in the South World the people of that place lived in a large house. They didn't have a regular fire in the center, but there were two Crows standing in the center, and when they cried, *"Ko'o'o'o'o'o,"* the fire came out of the ground, shooting sparks.

The two Rats peeked in at the door. Everybody was asleep. The two Rats steal on tiptoe, they step carefully, they make their way to the center of the house. They edge closer and closer to the Crows. They have their sticks of punkwood ready. The two Crows cry, *"Ko'o'o'o'o'o,"* the fire shoots up from the ground at their feet, the Woodrats catch the sparks in their punkwood and jump for the door.

Crane, they say, was the watchman at the door. He was asleep, lying stretched across the threshold. The Rats stumbled over his legs.

"Wa'a'a'k, Wa'a'a'k! Someone is stealing our fire!"

The people awoke on all sides.

"Are you all dead?" "What's the matter?" "Somebody stole a piece of our fire!" "Two of them did, the fire-stealers, those Woodrats." "Which way did they go?" "Here they are! Here they are!" "Catch them, hit them quick." "No, no, don't hit them. We'll keep them for pets." "Catch 'em!"

In the confusion the Rats slipped away under the leaves. Now the two fire-stealers were running back along the trail, back to the gate of the South World. *Tu-tu-tu-tu-tu,* the gate opened of itself toward the other side and they went through. They arrived at Coyote's house.

"Here, Grandfather, we have brought it." And they gave him the two sticks of punkwood. The fire was smouldering inside.

"Good," said Coyote. He took a piece of dry wood and scraped some fine shavings with a flint until he had a little pile, then he stuck the sticks into the pile and he blew on it.

"Some, smoke, smòke!" Then the fire blazed up and Hawk Chief was glad.

Coyote and his grandson the Hawk now had fire but it was dark all over the land. Hawk Chief began to gumble again.

"Grandfather, why haven't we a sun? I want sunlight, I want sunlight!"

"Yes, yes, I hear you, but how can I get it?!!"

"Oh, you know—you know everything, Grandfather, and how it used to be before the destruction of the world. You can get the sun if you want to."

"All right, all right, I'll go and see your cousins, the Doves. Maybe they can help us."

So the next day Coyote Old Man set out and, *ton-No-no-nono-nono,* he went south. He arrived at the house of the Dove brothers, then he called "Hey! Hey!"

One of the Doves answered from inside, "Well, the door is under the pepper tree. Can't you see it? You must be blind."

The other Dove scolded his brother.

"What's the matter with you? Haven't you *any* manners? *What* are you mad about now? *How* do you know but when you are mad like that *somebody* might be coming, someone who is Somebody, a chief of some tribe—and you acting like a FOOL. WHY, look, it's our Grandfather Coyote. There must be something wrong for Grandfather to be traveling so far from his home. Come IN, Grandfather, come IN. And why are you traveling?"

Coyote Old Man came in and sat down. He didn't say anything at first, then he took out his four sacks of beads and laid them on the ground before him. Then he took two sacks and laid them on the ground in front of one Dove, then he took two sacks and laid them in front of the other Dove. Then he said, "Why, I came because he wants the sun, your cousin. He grumbles all the time. He does not like it to be dark. That's what I want you two to do. I want you to get the sun—if you can."

"All right, Grandfather, all right. We think we can get the sun for you. Sure, yes, we'll start right away tomorrow."

"Yes, Grandfather, don't worry. We'll come by your place on our way. We'll surely be there, you can count on us. Yes, we'll get the sun for you. Yes, indeed."

"Good," said Coyote, and TONnonononono, he trotted back home.

Next morning they arrived.

"Well, grandfather, here we are, and what is it you want us to do?"

"Why, I want you to get the sun. The world is going

to be sunny all the time—it's going to be lighted. The Chief wants it that way."

"Oh, all right, all right, that's easy. Let's start right now."

So they started and they traveled away down south until they found the house of the sun. It lived there all alone in its house on top of a small hill. Grandfather Coyote and the two Doves stopped a little way off and they called. They called again, they called again, but the sun wouldn't come out.

"What are you going to do now?" Coyote asked. "How are you going to get it to come out?"

One of the Doves said to his brother, "You try first."

"No, you do it. YOU are the one."

"No, no, you do it. Go ahead, try it, anyhow. You can't do it, you are too young, but you can try first. THEN I'll show you how to do it."

"YOU? Why, you are too old. You are an old man already. You couldn't do it, you can't see. Look at me, I'm a young fellow, my eyes are good, my arm is strong."

"All RIGHT, then, go ahead and don't talk so much. WATCH him, Grandfather—and don't be afraid."

"Oh, I'm not afraid," said Coyote Old Man.

The younger Dove then took up his sling; he put a stone in it; then, they say, he sang four times,

Shunnera shunnera hu he kaa . . .

Then he whirled the sling above his head and let it go. Straight east went the stone and hit the house of the sun. The sun jumped high in the air through the smoke-hole, it hung there for a moment and then fell down again into the house.

"Well, well, well," said Coyote Old Man.

"Didn't I tell you?" said the older Dove to his brother. "Didn't I tell you? You did just as I said you would. Now watch me."

Then he started singing. He whirled the sling and let go. The stone went, went and crashed into the house of the sun, right in the middle of it. The sun jumped up through the smoke-hole, into the sky and there it stoppped still! "Well, well, well," cried Coyote Old Man.

The next evening Coyote Old Man continued his tale.

Now they had fire, and the sun shone over the world, but still Hawk Chief was not satisfied. He wandered around, grumbling.

"WHAT's the matter *now?*" asked his grandfather, the Coyote.

"Grandfather, WHY AREN'T THERE people? I want the world to have people."

This time Coyote Old Man got mad.

"All right," he said, "and then WE will have to go away!"

Then he carved some people out of little oak sticks but they did not become people.

Then he tried sticks of pine.

"Become people!" he ordered, but they did not become people.

He tried all kinds of trees but still they did not become people.

Coyote was mad. He cried, "When the fleas bite you, then you will become people."

The fleas bit them but that did not wake them up.

Then Coyote Old Man set to work; he took sticks of buckeye and carved all kinds of people out of them; he worked on them inside his ceremonial house, and then he set them up all around; he stuck them in the ground on the south side and on the north side and on the east side and on the west side. Then he cut up some milkweed into little pieces and scattered them all

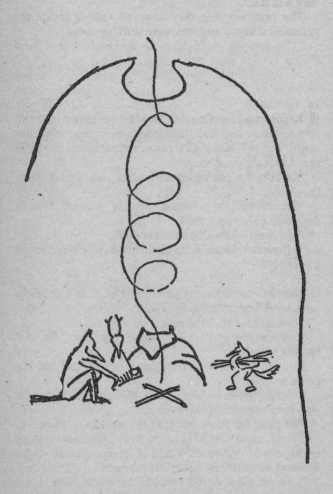

over the sticks, and he cried, "Tomorrow morning they will talk."

The next morning they were all talking inside the ceremonial house and they were walking about.

"The fleas nearly finished us last night," they were saying. Coyote came in and called to them.

"I want to speak to you all," he said, "and tell you who you are. Those who live in the west will be called by that name. Those who live in the south will talk in a different language. Those who live in the east will speak in a still different language. And those who live in the north will talk in still another. In the four lands there will be people now."

"The fleas finished us last night," they said.

"All right," said Coyote Old Man, "good morning, but now listen to me. I am not speaking about fleas, I am going to speak to you all and I am telling you something. I want to teach you. When that is done, in four days from now, I am going away. My grandson doesn't like it here."

"All right," the people said.

The next morning they woke up and started a dance. They danced four days. They were talking in different languages and they didn't understand one another.

Now Coyote spoke.

"When you die you are to come to my land, four days after you have died. Living people are NOT to come to my land: ONLY DEAD PEOPLE."

Then he went to work and arranged everything the way it was to be. He made the pine be pine, and the oak be oak. To Bluejay he said, "You are Bluejay," and to the Duck he said, "You are Duck." He said, "You are Deer," and "You are Mudhen." He made everything like that.

Then he called to his wife, she was Pelican Queen, "Old woman, hurry up now; gather up your things and your baskets. We are going now."

"Very well," said Pelican Queen.

Then he said to the people once more, "You all

heard what I said. Now, don't forget. When you die you are to come to my land in the west. In the west beyond the ocean, I shall be."

Hawk Chief wanted to stay, but the old man said, "Well, you wanted PEOPLE, didn't you. Now *we* have to go away. COME ALONG."

That's the way they went. They went away. They went west, beyond the ocean. That's where they live, and now the story is finished. . . .

The next morning while they were sitting around the fire eating acorn mush and rabbit ham and little round roasted balls made from the nuts of the laurel tree pounded into paste, Antelope and Bear started to argue. Bear said, "I don't understand how Coyote could make people as something new that had never been before, since he himself and Hawk and Flint and the Ducks and all the others were *already people*. That's too much for me."

Coyote Old Man just squinted and smiled and went on eating laurel-nut balls and rabbit ham, but Antelope said, "Aaah, you don't understand anything. He didn't say last night that his great-grandfather's grandfather made people, he said that Hawk complained because there were no people."

"Well, isn't that just what I was saying? *I* said that *you* said that *Grandfather* said—"

But Fox Boy interrupted, "Why don't you listen to the stories instead of talking like two magpies?"

"Well, what *does* the story say then, you smart boy?"

"How can I tell myself after you two have mixed it all up?"

At that Old Man Coyote burst out laughing and almost strangled on a rabbit bone.

"That boy is clever all right," he said. But Bear grumbled, "You are so clever yourself, Old Man, well then, tell me why you say that you made people when there were already people."

"Because I am Coyote Old Man. I am a very old

man. I am a thousand years old. I KNOW WHAT'S HAP-
PENED AFTER THE BEFORE and before the after!"

Bear growled, "That doesn't make sense what you
say," but Coyote shot back, "It doesn't make sense
to YOU because you are a young man yet, Mr. Bear.
You are too young yet to understand."

At that, Fox Boy started to dance. He whooped and
yelled and sang, "Father is too young, Father is too
young." He took Antelope by the hand and they both
danced around the fire singing, "Father is too young,
Father is too young."

Old Man Coyote got up and took the little baby
Quail in his arms and he joined the dance around the
fire. Bear growled, "Just a bunch of kids. I'm going
to hunt rabbits. Somebody has got to do something
useful in this camp."

"Wait a minute, Father, I'm going with you."

Antelope took up her weaving material; she had
commenced a new basket. Coyote was watching her.
He said, "Why don't you weave in the Quail pattern?"

"I don't know how it goes. Do you?"

"Yes, I'll show you how," and Old Man Coyote took
the basket from her. His fingers went fast, fast, fast.
Pretty soon you could see all the Quail running around
and around the basket, black figures on the white background.

"That's beautiful," said Antelope. Coyote gave her
back the basket and she continued weaving, but she
had to go slowly because it was a new pattern to her
and she often had to stop and ask instructions from
Old Man Coyote. Coyote was rocking the baby Quail
in her cradle-board.

"I'll sing the Quail song for you."

Daaabo le eeema ma a . . .

And now they were traveling along the trail again. Sometimes it went through the woods, and again it went through a patch of thick brush; the hills became real mountains and the trail wound in and out of canyons, sometimes under big trees, sometimes through chaparral. Finally they came to a good place to camp, in a little round valley with thick grass and a brook running through it. The sun was still high but they were so tired that they decided to stop and make camp and have a good rest.

The next morning Coyote Old Man, who had decided to go along with them, said, "We ought to stay here today. This is a nice place."

"But we have so far to go," Bear said. "We'll never get there at this rate."

"You'll never get anywhere. You're in too much of a hurry."

Antelope said, "Yes, that's right. We ought to stay here today. Our dried venison is getting low. We ought to stop here and you and Fox can go hunting—maybe get a deer. This should be good deer country. I'll dry the venison. Grandfather will cut up the meat, and I'll dry it over the fire."

"That's right," cried Fox, "Let's go hunting. I'll practice with my new spear."

So they both went, each his own way.

"You go west and I'll go east," Bear said, "and we'll both come back through the north. That way we will drive the deer toward each other."

Antelope cried after them, "Don't get lost again."

"Of course I won't," Fox shouted back. "I am a hunter . . . and anyhow, I have my magic flints with me."

Fox was stealing through the brush and chaparral, creeping around carefully, not making any noise, the way a good hunter does. He saw a big buck standing behind a tree. Fox could just see his rump through the brush. The big buck must be eating something on the ground because Fox couldn't see his head—but WHAT A RUMP! MUST be an elk!

Little Fox poises his spear in his hand carefully, he leans back, away down, almost until his hand touches the ground. He straightens up like a catapult and hurls the spear. He hits the mark, and a GRIZZLY bear stands up with a ROAR.

Fox jumped two feet in the air.

"Why, FATHER, WHAT are you doing here? I thought you were on the east side."

The grizzly bear shouted, "What's the idea of throwing a spear at me? . . . And I am NOT your father!"

Fox was bewildered.

"You are my father. Of course, you are my father. I'm sorry I threw that spear at you because I thought you were an elk—but you are my father just the same."

"I say I am NOT your father. What's the matter with you? Don't you know your own father?"

Just then a little girl came tripping up. She was just about the size of Fox and she was very pretty, with a little skirt of fibers, some black and others orange. She spoke to the grizzly bear.

"What's the matter, Father?"

"That boy threw a spear at me and he calls me 'Father.' I think he is crazy."

Fox looked at the little girl with great interest. She said to him, "You must not throw spears at people. It's not nice. And he is N-O-T your father. He is MY father."

Fox stamped his foot.

"He IS my father."

The little girl smiled at him and shook her head.

"No, he is not your father. I repeat, he is MY father. I think you are crazy, little boy, and you must NOT stamp your foot. It isn't nice. We don't allow people to stamp their foot in these mountains, or throw spears at people and call strangers 'Father.' "

Fox said, "What's your name?"

"My name is Oriole. What's yours?"

"I am Fox, and my father is Bear, and my mother is Antelope, and my little sister is Quail, and Grandfather Coyote has joined us and—"

The little girl interrupted, "That's all very interesting. Quite a family. Are you sure you are not crazy? As for me, I have no mother, only my father here . . ."

"He is NOT your father! He is MY father!!!"

"There he goes again," said Grizzly Bear. "Another fit! Plumb crazy!"

Fox cried, "It's you who are crazy . . . or maybe you are playing a joke on me, Father, but you are carrying it too far."

Grizzly Bear said, "Wait a minute. You say your people are camped down below?"

Fox Boy was getting mad. He cried, "Why, you know perfectly well where we are camped. You left me only a little while ago and you said, 'You hunt on the west side and I'll take the east side,' and we went each our way, and now you jump at me and say you are not my father. What kind of a joke is that?"

Oriole Girl interrupted him. "Father, maybe that little boy is not crazy after all. Maybe he really has people camped down there. We ought to go and investigate. He says his mother is Antelope. What's an antelope?"

"Oh, it's some kind of people like the deer. They live down in the valleys, down there in the country where I was born. . . . At least, that's what I've been told."

Fox drew himself up.

"Antelope is my mother *AND SHE IS VERY BEAUTIFUL.*"

Oriole Girl said, "Yes? It must be fun to have a mother. Father, let's go down there and investigate."

"All right, if this crazy boy will show the way." So they started.

"And what about that spear you threw at me? Are you going to leave it here?"

"Oooh, that's right." Fox went back and picked up his spear.

They started down the trail; Fox first, carrying his spear, then the Oriole Girl, then the Grizzly Bear.

Oriole said, "That's not the proper way to carry your spear, little boy."

"DON'T CALL ME A LITTLE BOY," shouted Fox. "And if you want my spear, I'll give it to you and you can show me how to carry it."

Grizzly Bear roared with laughter.

They went down and down the trail and arrived at the camp. Antelope was there alone, weaving a basket. She said, "Well, did you get a deer? And who is that little girl?"

"No, we didn't get a deer, and that boy threw a spear at me, and that little girl is my daughter. And who are you?"

Antelope dropped her basket in her astonishment.

"Who am I, you ask? And you say that little girl is your daughter? What's the matter with you? Are you crazy?"

Fox cried, "And he says he is not my father."

The Grizzly Bear said to Antelope, "Maybe you also are crazy like the little boy. Do you throw spears at people and call them 'father'?"

"I don't throw spears at anyone or anything, AND I don't call you 'father' but 'HUSBAND,' AND I haven't any children hidden around. *How long* have you been hiding that child? . . . And why didn't you tell me before???"

"Plumb crazy!" said the Grizzly Bear, shaking his head. "Just like the little boy who threw a spear at me. Listen! I am NOT your husband. I never saw you before. And who is that old man coming there? Is he also going to throw a spear at me and call me HIS father, or his husband, or his wife, maybe? Oh, I KNOW that old man. He is Grandfather Coyote."

And just at that moment the other Bear arrived, carrying a deer on his shoulders. Both children ran to him, calling him 'FATHER.'

"Hello," said Bear; then he went and dropped his load in front of the camp fire. Then he looked for a long time at the other Bear, then he sat down on a log and started to laugh and laugh.

The other Bear said, "One more crazy one. Grandfather Coyote, who are these crazy people?"

Antelope was looking from one bear to the other in utter bewilderment.

"Which is which?" she murmured.

Bear was laughing so hard that he couldn't speak for a moment. Finally, he said, "I'll tell you. This man is my twin brother. At least I think he is. I've been thinking about it ever since we met that Chipmunk back there. You remember how he spoke about a big man who lived all alone in these mountains with his daughter and he looked like me? Well, you see, you know how among our people they don't like twins and they always get rid of one of them somehow or other. We were twins, and they gave my brother away—my mother told me about it when I was a little boy. They gave him away to some relatives who lived a long way off with some other tribe. . . ."

"That's right," said Grizzly Bear. "They told me the same thing when I was a little boy, then when I grew up I forgot all about it. So you are my brother. Well, well, well."

Now they all went to work cutting up the deer to make it into jerky and dry it by the fire and in the sun.

They spent the whole afternoon cutting the meat with knives of obsidian flint. Fox and Oriole were helping, too. *But everybody kept getting the Bears mixed up.* The two Bears themselves were the only ones who did not get confused; they each knew which was which. Finally, Antelope said, "This won't do. I must be able to tell you two apart, otherwise, I'm likely to think the wrong one is my husband."

"I know a way," Oriole said. "My Father Bear can wear a string of beads around his neck, then I can tell which is my Uncle Bear."

"That's a bright girl," said Coyote Old Man, and reaching into his sack he brought out a string of warrior beads, a warrior's necklace.

"Thank you, thank you, Grandfather," said Grizzly Bear.

His brother grumbled, "You were always the lucky one."

"All right," said Grizzly, "If you are not satisfied, we can trade. You take these beads and I'll take your wife."

"That's all right, Brother. You keep the beads, they look too nice on you. I wouldn't deprive you of them."

They had not finished cutting up all the meat from the deer and drying it, so the next day they stayed in the same camp. Fox Boy and Oriole Girl got tired of cutting up meat, and cutting up meat, and cutting up meat, so they went off to play.

"I'll show you how to throw a spear," said Fox. "See that stump? It's a deer." He threw his spear and missed the stump by a couple of feet.

"Not bad for a little boy," Oriole said. "You'll learn with practice."

"Well, you throw it, then, you great big woman!" Fox did not know that all these mountaineers were adept with the spear. Oriole took it, poised herself, threw it, and the spear stuck into the stump, quivering.

"Deer, shot right through the heart! That's the way we do it," Oriole shouted.

Fox whistled in admiration, "Say, you are good at it, girl!"

"Sure, I am. I've been throwing spears since I was a baby."

"I bet you couldn't use bow-and-arrows."

"Bet you I could. Let me have your bow-and-arrows and I'll show you."

"I haven't a bow-and-arrows, I lost mine, but I think Father will let me borrow his."

So they went back to the camp.

"*HariKa!* May I borrow your bow-and-arrows?"

"All right, but take only one arrow. You are always losing them."

But that was a strong, stiff bow of Bear's, and Fox Boy was not able to string it. He tried and tried, but he could not bend it enough to slip the loop of the bow string over the end of the bow. Oriole helped him, and by both of them pulling hard they finally managed to string the bow.

Now, Fox was fairly good with that kind of tool and he hit close to the target. But it was new to Oriole. In fact, she could not shoot at all; she did not know how to keep the nock of the arrow in the string, and when she pulled and let the arrow fly, it simply fell at her feet and the bow string hit her a smart blow on the wrist.

So the children practised all day. Oriole showed Fox how to hold the spear properly balanced and how to bend his body backward, then sweep the arm in a circle and let go the spear at the proper moment.

"Anyhow, your spear isn't fixed properly. You should have a thong tied to the middle part of the spear and swing the spear by the thong, like a handle. I'll ask my father to fix it."

· So Grizzly Bear fixed it, and now Fox could throw the spear much farther, but it still went far off the target. And Oriole finally learned to hold the nock of the arrow in the string properly, and when the arrow finally went, it hit Grizzly square when he was bending to turn the jerky over.

"What a life! First, they throw spears at you, and then they shoot you full of arrows!"

The next morning they were all getting ready to go and packing their things. Oriole was cleaning the baby Quail, Fox was helping her, and Antelope was packing the jerky. Bear was straightening some arrow shafts— he rubbed them hard through a hole in a piece of wood to make the shaft hot by friction, then he squinted down the length of the shaft, and if it had a bend, he straightened it. Coyote Old Man was going around the camp, poking at things with his walking-stick.

"Mustn't leave any trash around, especially nothing that you have handled a good deal. If an enemy should find it he could use it for magic against you." Coyote Old Man was careful; he knew all the rules.

But Grizzly sat on a log and looked sad.

"I hate to see you all go. It will be lonesome again after you go."

"Well, why don't you come along with us, Brother? It will do you good to travel. Look at me, I am still young and strong because I travel."

"Listen, Brother, I am just as young as you are, and I have done a powerful lot of traveling when I was younger. I have lived with almost every tribe from here on north. But since my woman died I haven't gone anywhere."

Antelope said, "How do you expect to find another woman if you live all alone in the woods?"

Then Oriole Girl spoke up. "Oh, let's go, Father. I haven't anybody to play with here. Let's go with them."

61

"Well, all right then, we'll go. But first of all we'll have to go by our place and clean the house. It's not far from here."

So they all started. Grizzly had said that it was not far. He and Oriole were used to the mountains and they went along at a good clip without stopping to catch their breath, although Grizzly carried a lot of the provisions as his pack. The Bear family were lagging far behind, that is, Coyote, Bear, and Antelope, because Fox Boy was keeping up with the other two and jog-trotting uphill. But he didn't have time to throw his spear at anything, he had all he could do to keep up with Oriole. When the others arrived at last, it was late afternoon. They had their supper and then they all went to bed.

The next morning they started packing early. But first of all they cleaned Grizzly's house. They took out all the tule reeds that served as a carpet and they burned them, then they gathered all the cooking baskets and hung them from the rafters. Last, Grizzly took his comb made from a porcupine's tail and hung it from a rafter by tying it at the end of a string.

"That's the proper way to leave a house—it means you are coming back. If the comb falls, if the string that ties it to the rafter breaks and the comb falls, that means you are not coming back because you have had bad luck and you are dead."

And now they started on the trail, *tras . . . tras . . . tras. . . .* They made quite a big party, with Fox Boy and Oriole Girl in the lead, then Grandfather Coyote with his walking staff, then Antelope with the baby Quail on her back, and last the Bears carrying heavy packs.

Before they started Oriole had tried to get Fox's magic flints away from him. They had gone to bed together under the same rabbit-skin blanket, and in the dawn, while they were singing for their shadows to come home, she had begged him to lend her his flints.

"No, I can't," he had said. "They are magic flints. The Chief of the Flint people gave them to me, and he said I must use them only if I should be in trouble."

"You are a selfish little boy," and she had turned her back on him.

So when they stopped for lunch, Fox went to Coyote.

"Grandfather, will you give me a string of beads?"

"I haven't' any beads. I gave them all to your uncle."

"Oh, yes, Grandfather, you still have some. All you have to do is to open your little sack and there are always beads in it."

Coyote laughed and gave him a string of beads. Fox gave them to Oriole.

"Here. I am not selfish."

"Oh, thank you, thank you, big boy." (But she had made up her mind to get his flints from him.)

When they started on the trail again Fox and Oriole did not always stay with the rest of the party. They were practicing with their slings so they often let the rest get out of sight before they started to run and catch up, and sometimes they took short cuts through brush or over small ridges. AND THAT'S THE WAY THEY GOT LOST—*completely lost.* They could not find the trail at all, they just did not know where they were.

Fox Boy began to have the HA-HAS, but Oriole Girl mimicked him and made fun of him.

"That won't help us, crying and getting scared. But you are a valley boy; mountain people are used to getting lost. Why don't you do the way you did that time before when you got lost? What about your magic flints? Shoot one of them into the sky and maybe he'll tell us which way to go."

"I haven't got my bow-and-arrows."

"Put a flint in your sling and shoot it, silly!"

"Oh, yes, I can do that," said Fox Little Boy.

Oriole said under her breath, "Strong back, strong back, Mister Strong Back."

"What did you say?" asked Fox.

"I didn't say anything. Shoot your sling."

Fox took one of the flints out of his little sack, put it in the sling, whirled the sling, and let it go. The flint went up, up, up, away up, and then came down. Fox picked it up and put it to his ear.

"He says he saw a house on the other side of that ridge."

"Well, let's go then. What are you waiting for?"

"It's a pretty high ridge."

"Oh, come on, you valley boy. You have to get used to the mountains."

So the children climbed the ridge. It was stiff climbing, and Oriole let Fox help her over the rocks—it pleased him so much. They got to the top of the ridge at last and below they saw a blue lake, a mountain lake, deep blue, almost black. Tule reeds grew along the shore, and they could see a small house half-hidden in the tules. It looked lonesome.

"Well, let's go down there and ask our way."

But Fox would not go; he sat on a log and looked uneasy.

"I don't like to go down there—it might be dangerous."

"Oh, all you need now is a stone pipe, Mister Tamat'-He—old Pine Marten! I am going down there. You can wait for me here."

She ran down the cliff, jumping from rock to rock, her black and orange skirt billowing around her. Fox Boy thought she looked very pretty.

When Oriole reached the shore of the lake she stopped and listened—she thought she heard someone calling. No, there was no one calling, but that house half hidden in the tules—she was afraid of it. Something might be lurking there. What thing? But it might know the way out for her and Fox Boy.

Then again she heard that weird cry from the middle of the lake.

"That's someone calling me, I think." She tiptoed, she peered, she separated the stalks of the tule reeds and peered. She could not see anything and yet, at that very moment, she heard the weird cry again. The sun was high, the lake was full of sunlight. Oriole said, "It's IMPOSSIBLE."

She was not afraid in the least when she stepped into that house half hidden in the tules. It was a house, rare in the north country, with a door at the side, facing the lake, instead of a smoke-hole.

She went; she went in the doorway; she stepped in. She heard the Center Post talking to the Main Rafter.

"Our mother is stranded in the middle of the lake. Her boat capsized. She is too old to swim to the shore. She just managed to get to that rock in the middle of the lake and cling to it . . . and now she is crying for help."

The Fire said, "Then why don't you go and help her?"

The Center Post answered, "I can't. The house would

fall down if I did not support it. But you, why don't you go?"

The Fire answered, "I would be no use in the lake. The moment I stepped into the water I would die."

Oriole called from the doorway, "Whose house is this?"

"It is old woman Loon's house. She ought not to go out fishing alone any longer. She is too old."

"Isn't there another boat around here?"

"Yes, there is. See there, hidden in the tules."

Oriole got into the boat and paddled out to the rock in the middle of the lake.

"Thank you, thank you, child. Take these beads. They come from the sea. Hide them in your skirt— don't show them to anyone—keep them secret—but if you should be in trouble, drop them into the water, and someone will come and help you."

And she gave Oriole a string of abalone shell pearls, beautiful and iridescent in the sunlight.

"THANK YOU, thank you, Grandmother."

Oriole climbed the mountainside again and there she found Fox Boy sound asleep on the log where she had left him.

"Well, did you find out anything?"

"Yes, Mister Pine Marten. That house was full of Digging-Stick old women and they told me that we should go down this canyon." And she started down the draw.

"Hey, wait for me. I don't believe you. You never saw any Digging-Stick old women. You don't know where you are going. We'll get lost again. Oriole, Oriole, wait, wait. . . ."

But she was running licketysplit down the canyon, laughing and jumping from rock to boulder. She arrived at the bottom where the canyon emerged into a narrow valley with a stream flowing through the center. She stepped into the stream, and unfastening the string of abalone pearls under her skirt she dropped it into the water. Immediately the string of pearls began to swim upstream like a wriggling watersnake.

Oriole grabbed it again, tied it under her skirt and sat down to wait for Fox. Soon he arrived, out of breath. Oriole started upstream.

"COME ON."

"Hey, wait, Oriole. I'm sure you are going the wrong way. It can't be upstream." But she did not argue, she went on, with him following.

In no time they arrived at another valley with a well-marked trail and just at that moment the Bear party came in sight around the bend, Grizzly, and Bear, and Antelope, and Old Man Coyote.

"Well, you laggards," Fox cried. "You certainly are slow people. We have been waiting here for days for you to catch up."

They camped that evening in a small round valley. The next day at the noontime rest, Old Man Coyote said, "Let's camp here for the rest of the day. My moccasins are all worn out; I need to make new ones. We ought to find enough flat tule reeds somewhere on this stream to weave me a new pair of slippers."

So they ate and Coyote Old Man went in search of tules. Antelope took the basket with the quail design out of her pack and settled down to work on it. The bears dug for roots.

Oriole Girl said to Fox Boy, "Let's you and I go upstream and see what we can find."

"No, I don't want to go with you. You'll get me into trouble again. I am going to dig for roots."

"All right, little boy, but don't eat too many cascara berries. They are not good for little boys. I am going upstream to find me some nice big boys to play with."

Oriole followed the bank of the stream for quite a way until she arrived at a small lake. Some Beaver people had made a village there; they had made the lake by building a dam across the stream. Their house was in the middle of the lake. There did not seem to be any smoke-hole and neither was there a door. Oriole looked at it curiously and wondered how they got in.

Some Beaver boys were playing water polo not far from the bank.

"Come here and play with me, big boys."

"You come here and play with us. We are water people. We don't feel at home on land. Come here and join us."

"I cannot swim."

"That's too bad, but we don't care. We are water people and you are a land person. We don't feel at home on land. Come here and join us."

"But I can't swim!"

"That's too bad, but we don't care. We are water people and you are a land person." They resumed their play and paid no more attention to her.

Oriole thought, "All right, you selfish little boys. I'll make you look at me." She took the abalone pearls from under her skirt and she put them around her neck. It was not long before a Beaver boy came up out of the water and sat on the bank next to her.

"What pretty beads you have."

"You like them?"

"Oh, yes, they are so beautiful. Let me borrow them, I want to show them to my mother."

Oriole gave him the string of abalone pearls with a smile. He dove into the water with a whoop and a yell, and all the Beaver boys after him. Under the water he called, "Hey, boys, hey, boys, we fooled the land person. We got her beads. Come on, come on, let's divide them."

Oriole Girl was going around the lake crying. On the bank on the other side a woman was sitting, fishing.

"Why do you cry, little girl?"

"They stole my beads, those boys, those Beaver boys!"

"What kind of beads were they?"

"A string of abalone pearls."

The woman looked at her suspiciously.

"Where did you get such beads? Only we water people have that kind, but you, you are a land person."

"An old woman gave them to me because she was stranded in the lake and I went with a boat and brought her to the shore. She lives over there, not far, on the other side of the mountain."

"Yes, I know her. She is my grandmother and she ought not to be living alone, she is too old. But, tell me, did she not tell you something special when she gave you the beads?"

"Yes, she told me never to show them to anyone unless I was in trouble."

"Then why did you show them to those boys?"

"Because they wouldn't play with me."

The woman said, "I don't call THAT being in trouble. SERVES YOU RIGHT," and she went back to her fishing.

But Oriole kept crying and crying.

"You say that because you are a grown person and you don't know what it is to be a little girl and the boys won't play with you."

The woman stopped fishing again.

"But I do remember. Listen, I TAKE PITY ON YOU, I will help you because you helped one of our people. They call us CRAZY LOONS but you, a land person, helped one of us, so I will help you. Jump on my back, put your arms around my neck, hold on tight and DON'T BE AFRAID." The woman slid off the bank into the water and she swam out to the middle of the lake with little Oriole hanging onto her neck. They were getting close to that house of the Beaver boys. The woman warned Oriole, "I am going to dive under the water right into their house. The door is underneath. Hold your breath for an instant. Hold on tight. Here we go."

They went under. The water swished past Oriole, past her ears; water glassy, dark, darker. Suddenly they shot up and out of the water inside the house of the Beavers. Loon and Oriole jumped onto the platform of sticks where all the Beaver boys were sitting in a circle around the necklace of abalone pearls. They were playing handgame for it. They gave one yell together, "The crazy Loon, the witch. Save yourselves!" They all dived into the water and disappeared.

The old woman picked up the beads and gave them to Oriole.

"Thank you, oh, thank you, Sister."

"And next time, take better care of them."

"Yes, my elder Sister."

"Now, get on my back again, and hold on tight. We are plunging out of here."

When they reached the shore Oriole took her own necklace of clamshell beads and put them around the Loon's neck.

"Thank you, thank you, younger Sister."

"Take this fish with you for your people."

As Oriole started back downstream, the Beaver boys mocked her from the water.

"She is a land person, She is a land person. She can't swim."

Oriole made a face at them and went on. When she reached the camp, Fox asked her, "Where did you get the fish?"

She said, "In a tree." She gave the fish to Antelope.

Fox said, "She says she got them in a tree!" Antelope gave Oriole a sidelong look, she saw that the necklace of clamshell beads was gone, but she didn't say anything. She skewered the fish on a long stick and started to broil them over the fire.

The bears and Coyote arrived on different trails, the bears loaded with fresh roots. Coyote Old Man was not packing anything, he came in limping on his stick. Then he sniffed, "I SMELL FISH. Fish! Oh fine." He was there at the head of the line with his little basket.

Coyote Old Man said, "Oh, but that fish tastes good. I haven't had a fish for a long time."

Fox said, "Grandfather, do trees ever grow on fishes—I mean do fishes ever grow on trees?"

Everybody roared with laughter, and Coyote choked on a fishbone—they had to slap him on the back. In the confusion Oriole whispered fiercely to Fox, "Can't you keep quiet? IF YOU FIND trees at the bottom of the water then you always find fish growing on them."

Fox gave her a wink. "Go get yourself another fish," he said, and he went to the fire and helped himself to another big chunk.

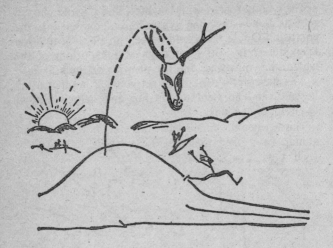

After supper the children demanded another story. Grizzly said, "All right, I'll tell you the story of Weasel and the deer-head decoy. But, first of all I must tell you what a deer-head decoy is. It's a stuffed deer head that you wear on your own head in order to fool the deer when you go out hunting. You skin the head of the deer and stuff it with straw and when you see a herd of deer grazing in the distance you strap the decoy on your own head and get down on your hands and knees and creep along as if you were grazing. Deer don't see very well, as long as you keep to the leeward of them so they don't smell you.

"But you must not play with a decoy or you will spoil its charm, make it lose its power. A good hunter never lets anyone touch his hunting tools, his bow, his arrows, his spear, and it holds true for the deer-hand decoy also. Well, here's the story."

. . . Pine Marten and his little brother, the Weasel, were living with the Marten's woman and her folk.

The Marten's woman was Frog—her father was Coyote. The Weasel, he never could get a woman for himself. His real name is "Yas," but some people call him the "Diniki." (That word, "Diniki," doesn't mean anything—just a name—but it always makes him mad when you call him that.)

The Marten, his name is Tamat'He. He is kind of slow and deliberate and he smokes an old stone pipe.

The Marten's woman was sick. Her mother, the old woman Frog, said to him, "That girl is sick. Maybe she'll die. I can do nothing. You go and see my younger sister, the one who lives at the end of the valley at Tulu'qupi. She has great power, that one."

Tamat'He, the Pine Marten, left in the morning, but before he went he said to the Weasel, "Listen, you! My woman is sick. That's why I have had no luck hunting. I am going to the end of the valley to get that doctor, the old woman Frog's sister. She has power, that one, and maybe she can help. I'll be gone one, two, three days, maybe four, five days—I don't know. I don't want you to come along, you always make trouble. Those people are strangers—you would make trouble.

"Now listen, you Diniki, behave yourself while I am gone. Help around the camp, bring in firewood for the old woman, and leave my bow-and-arrows alone. Don't play with the deer-head decoy. Those are hunter's tools, not little boy's playthings. Now I go."

That was a long speech for Marten. Then he left.

Pine Marten and Weasel, they were brothers, and they always traveled together, they had gone all over the world together, but this time the Marten traveled alone.

After the Marten was gone Weasel did not do anything to help around the camp; he never brought in firewood for old woman Frog, he never helped pound acorns for the soup. He went out hunting lizards on the flats. He was angry. He said, "You can't catch lizards without bow-and-arrows. My brother wants me to help. I am trying to catch lizards for the soup, but you can't catch lizards without a bow-and-arrows. To the devil with it!"

He went around the camp grumbling, but nobody paid any attention to him, they were worried about the sick girl. He got up in the morning, he took the bow-and-arrows, he took the deer-head decoy and went out across the flats to a butte and there he played all day. He threw the deer head high into the air and then ran down the hill, shooting arrows at it. He did like that all day, throwing the deer head high in the air, shooting arrows at it.

"I am a hunter, that's what I am!"

When the sun was getting low in the sky and he was getting tired, it was lonely out there on the flats. Time to go home.

"I'LL TRY ONE MORE THROW."

He drew the deer head decoy high into the sunset. When it came down that time IT WAS GRINNING. Weasel did not shoot, he threw down the bow-and-arrows. He runs, he is running home over the flats, crying. AND THE DEER HEAD IS CHASING HIM. It is a big elk running after him.

He was nearly home, but the elk got him. The elk picked him up on his antlers and then he turned around and went up to the hills with the Weasel on his head.

Tamat'He, the Marten, came home.

"Where is my little brother?"

"Your little brother is gone. It's not our fault. The big deer took him to the mountains."

Marten sat down and cried. Frog Old Woman came to him.

"Is my sister coming?"

"Yes, she is coming. She'll be here tomorrow." Tamat'He was crying.

The old woman's sister arrived. She was a powerful doctor. She went into the brush, she was singing in the brush all day. Then she went to Marten.

"Why do you cry for your brother? He is good for nothing, that Weasel, but it hurts me to see you cry and I will help you to get him back, that Yas, that Diniki."

Tamat'He was crying.

That woman, she was a *tsigitta'waalu,* a real old-time woman doctor. She said to Marten, "Now, listen to me. When I make him come he will be on the antlers of the big deer. Then YOU SHOOT HIM, you understand? Shoot your brother, NOT the deer!"

Then she made all the rest but Marten go down into the underground house but she stayed on the roof with Marten. She danced—she made a great storm gather over the mountains. Lightning and thunder and RAIN in torrents—rain, rain, RAIN.

The waters were coming down from the hills, down the gullies and the canyons. All the animals were fleeing before the waters, all the deer from the mountains, their hoofs making a great noise and their antlers clashing. At their head came a big mule deer, and the Diniki was holding on to his antlers, crying with fear.

Tamat'He strung an arrow. He slowly took aim.

"No, DON'T SHOOT THE DEER! Shoot your brother. Shoot your brother!"

Tamat'He lets fly. The arrows goes through the Diniki, it knocks him off the antlers of the big deer. He rolls to the ground, and the elk lopes off to the mountains.

Tamat'He picked up the body of his little brother and held him upside down while the old woman doctor picked sagebrush twigs and whipped the Weasel with them. He came back to life, the Diniki, the Weasel. He sat up, he rubbed his eyes and looked around.

"Well, Brother, I see you got back. While you were gone I went into the mountains and tracked a big deer.

If I had had a bow-and-arrows I would have shot him sure—but I'll take you to the place tomorrow."

Marten sat on a log, smoking his stone pipe. He did not answer.

When they got up the next morning, Antelope looked at Bear and said, "I don't see how your shadow recognized you this morning. YOUR FACE IS ALL SWOLLEN!! What did you do yesterday, play with a witch while you were digging for roots?"

"I guess it must be POISON OAK," Bear said. "My face and neck itch like the devil!"

His face was all puffed up; you could barely see his eyes.

Grizzly said, "My, but you look funny, Brother. You look like one of the sausage people in the story. Let me take a pine needle and prick you to let the juice out."

Coyote Old Man said, "Maybe you ate too many berries yesterday."

Fox said, "Maybe it was the fish."

Bear lost his patience.

"There are too many doctors here. If you all keep on talking like that what I'll get is a bad case of the HA-HAS. If we were at home I could make a sweat bath and that would be the best thing for me."

Grizzly said, "Well, why don't you make a sweat bath here?"

"How can I? We have no house here. At home we make a hot fire inside the house, then we close the door and the smoke-hole and we sweat and sweat. Then when we are good and hot, so hot we can hardly stand it, we run out and plunge into the creek. That's the way we do down there."

"Well, around here and up north, we do differently.

77

We make a little house of willow branches, a little round hut just big enough for one person to sit inside, then we heat a lot of rocks over a fire outside. When they are red hot, we pile them up in a corner inside the little hut, then you go in with a small basket of water and sit and sprinkle a little water on the hot rocks. Swishhh, up goes the steam. You boil yourself until you can't stand it any more, then you run out and plunge into the creek and feel like a young buck."

Antelope said, "That's a good idea. Let's try it. Let's camp here all day and we'll all take steam baths. I can't let my husband go on with the HA-HAS."

"It's NOT the HA-HAS!" roared Bear.

Fox said, "Well, it may not be the HA-HAS, but it surely SOUNDS like it."

Grizzly said, "Come on, children, let's go and gather willow branches. Grandfather Coyote can be the fire-tender. It takes a lot of firewood for heating the rocks, you know, and my sister-in-law can bring in the rocks. My brother can sit and suck his paws until we get his bath ready."

Bear growled, "Will you leave me alone! I'll get the rocks. I don't have to use my face to gather rocks."

So the children went off with Grizzly.

"Will you make me a bow, Uncle Grizzly?" Fox asked. "Then I won't have to borrow Father's bow all the time."

"Sure, I'll make you a bow, but first find me a good piece of yew wood."

"What does the tree look like, Uncle? Like a pine tree?"

"No, like a fir tree; but you'll know it from a fir because instead of cones it bears red berries. The bird people like the berries."

"May I go and look for a yew tree?"

"All right, but don't get lost."

When Fox got back to the camp, Oriole asked him, "Where did you get that piece of bow wood?"

Fox squinted and answered, "I found it at the bottom of the creek. That's the way it grows, under water."

Grizzly was coming out of the steam bath.

"That's fine! That's fine bow wood, good yew wood, just right. That will make three bows, one for me, one for you and one for Oriole. Now, run into the little sweating house and take a bath. The rocks are still hot. The water is in a basket inside."

Antelope said, "And what about me? Don't I get a bow too?"

"Sister-in-law, you don't need a bow. Your wit is sharp enough to kill anything—even a bear."

"Maybe, but it has never penetrated my husband yet."

Bear was dozing in the sun with fern leaves over his face. He pretended not to hear.

So Fox went into the little hut of willow branches, and Oriole squeezed in too. There was a rabbit-skin blanket spread over the door hole. At first it was so dark inside that the children could not see anything, but in a little while their eyes got accustomed to it. Then Fox felt for the basket of water and sprinkled the rocks. *Hwishhhhhhhh* went up the stream. Antelope peeked in.

"Don't make too much steam or you'll scald yourselves."

That evening Fox Boy asked, "Uncle Grizzly, tell us the story of Erikanner and Erihutiki."

"All right. . . ."

. . . Erikanner and his younger brother, Erihutiki, lived together. They were great deer hunters. They set a deer-lane trap. Erihutiki drives the deer to the trap. He shouts "Hey, hey, hey" as he drives the deer toward the trap.

Erikanner was waiting in ambush. He let all the deer pass through, then he got up and shot the last one in the rear. The arrow went through all the line and came out of the leader's mouth. All the deer fell down, dead.

Then Erikanner ran along the line and with his foot he broke off the antlers of the bucks to change them into does. When Erihutiki arrived he said, "This is funny. There were a lot of bucks in that bunch, and here they are all does. Yes, I am sure they were nearly all bucks. Have you done anything to them, Brother?"

"No."

They packed the carcases home, they cut them up into strips, they dried them into jerky, but all night long Erihutiki was thinking and wondering. Next morning he got up in the dawn and sneaked off to hunt alone. He shot a big buck and brought it home. He cut him up and roasted him on the fire.

"My brother played a trick on me—my older brother played a trick on me. Brother, come and eat. This meat is good."

But Erikanner sat in his camp, he would not come.

A little dog appeared in Erihutiki's camp, a little striped dog. He had smelled the roasting fat.

"Oh, Erikanner, look! A little dog."

Erikanner sat in his camp—he did not answer.

Erihutiki feeds the little dog. He pets the little striped dog. Every morning he feeds the little dog.

"Oh, Erikanner, look! The little dog is growing fat. He is growing horns. He is growing big."

Erikanner sat in his camp—he did not answer.

"Oh, Erikanner, the little dog has bitten me!"

Erikanner sat in his camp—he did not answer.

Now the monster hooked Erihutiki on his horns and he went away to the hills with him.

"Oh, Erikanner, he is taking me away, he is taking me away!"

Erikanner did not answer. He was hiding in his camp. He was afraid of the monster. He was hiding in his camp crying, "Yakak, yakak, yakak!"

In the spring Erikanner put on a mourning for his little brother, he smeared his head with pitch and ashes and then he started, following the tracks of the monster. As he was crossing a flat he heard Meadow Lark singing:

"Erikanner's brother, they are going to kill him, twi, twi.

They are going to kill him, twi, twi."

Erikanner stuck his cane in the ground. The cane was smeared with pitch. Meadow Lark came and perched on the cane and stuck in the pitch. Erikanner tore him to pieces.

"From now on you'll be nothing but a meadowlark!" And he went on, crying, *"Yakak, yakak yakak!"*

He arrived at Spider's house.

"Aunt Spider, you who know everything, you who make your net everywhere, have you heard where my brother is?"

"Yes, I will tell you. Over there he is, on the other side of the river. When you reach this side of the river you must talk to Badger Old Man who is splitting firewood on this side. You must kill him, but only after you have questioned him. Here are little mice— take them. Here is a snake—take him. Here are tule reeds—take them."

And Erikanner went on. At night he arrived on this side of the river. Ahead of him he heard somebody splitting firewood, *Tul, tul, tul, tul*. It was Old Man Badger splitting firewood.

"Where do you come from? Where are you going?"

"Oh, I am just traveling downstream. And you, why are you splitting so much wood?"

"I am the fire-tender."

"And who lives here?"

"Some people live here, and they are going to have a dance."

"Why are they going to have a dance?"

"They are keeping Erikanner's brother and maybe he will soon die."

"Whereabouts are they keeping him?"

"In a basket over the smoke-hole. They have him hanging up there, and he is getting dried up, he is getting dried up. Pretty soon he will be dead. That's why I am splitting firewood, to keep the fire going under him. He is taking a very long time to die, Erikanner's brother, crying all the time, but he is drying nicely and before long he will be dead."

"And how are you going to get across the river?"

"When I am ready I will call 'SHOVE THE BOAT ACROSS.' Then I jump into the boat and when the boat starts to rock, I cry, 'I AM NOT A STRANGER.' "

"Then what do you do when you reach the other side? Are you not afraid that these people might kill you?"

"I jump through the smoke-hole into the house and first thing I drink some hot water, then I close my eyes and I say, 'MY HEART IS COOKED!' That's what I do. Now we have talked long enough. Help me pack the wood!"

Now Erikanner got up. He killed old man Badger, then he dressed himself in Badger's skin. Now he looked like Badger himself.

"SHOVE THE BOAT ACROSS!" he called, and the boat came across of itself. He jumped into the boat and when it started to rock, he cried, "I am not a stranger." When the boat arrived at the other shore, he jumped out and ran to the house. He ran up the roof and down the smoke-hole ladder. He drank the hot water, closed his eyes and said, "My heart is burning."

But as he jumped into the house he had grabbed his little brother, Erihutiki, from the basket where he was drying up over the smoke-hole and had hidden him in his bosom.

And now someone said, "Are you, perhaps, Erikanner?" but he sneaked off quietly without answering. As he was going out he turned the little mice loose inside the house, and as he was going out he scattered the little pieces of tule reeds all over the floor, and as he was going out the smoke-hole he left the little snake sitting there by the smoke-hole; he sat there, the little snake, shooting out his tongue.

The people of the house cried, "Look at the lightning! It means that strangers are coming for war." So they went to bed prepared. They tied knives to their wrists and then they went to sleep.

As the people sleep, all ten of them, the mice scatter punkwood around and pitch, punkwood and pitch and broken bits of tule reeds.

The sleepers are fast asleep. The little mice tie them together by their long hair. When dawn came they set fire to the house.

"HA, HA, HA, the strangers are coming!!!"

The people all jump up to fight together, tied by their hair. They are stabbing each other in the darkness. That's the way they killed one another and all of them burned up with the house. . . .

Fox Boy said, "Grandfather Coyote, are you sure you did not get mixed up in your story the other day? Are you sure that Erikanner was a pine marten?"

"I never told you that Erikanner was a marten! It's your Uncle Grizzly who told you that story."

"But you say that Tamat'He, the Marten, was the elder brother of Yas, the Weasel, and Coyote was the younger brother of Silver Fox who was your great-great-grandfather—I mean my great-great-grandfather. Oh, oh, oh, I am getting all mixed up! I don't know any more which is which and which is what!"

"Yes," said Coyote Old Man, "it's just like your mother who can't tell which is her husband and which is her brother-in-law. . . ."

"NOT AT ALL," said Antelope. "I know perfectly well which is which; one has a collar of beads and the other has the grouch."

Oriole said to Fox, "Oh, come along and let's play. You study too much; it will hurt your back. Why do you ask all those questions from the grown-ups? They don't know the answers. You only embarrass them."

"But I want to know the truth."

"What for?"

"Because I want to know the way it really happened."

"IT HAPPENED THE WAY they tell it."

"But they tell it differently!"

"Then it is because it happened differently."

Fox looked at Oriole sidewise. "How do you know

85

so much? You are not bigger than I am. You said yourself that I have a strong back."

"Oh, yes, Big Boy, you have a very strong back!"

Fox gave her a suspicious look, then he said, "At least I do not look for fish in the tops of the trees."

"AND I do not look for yew trees under the water. Come on, let's not quarrel like the grown-ups; let's go and play."

In the camp Grizzly was working on the pieces of yew wood, scraping them thin in order to make them into bows. He was making them northern-fashion, flat and wide, and not much longer than three feet, and very flexible. He was scraping them with a flint and every little while he squinted down the length to see if the bow was straight.

Bear's face was still swollen with poison oak, but not as much as before. He was watching Grizzly.

"You'd better be careful, Brother, you are getting the white sap wood too thin. You have to keep as much white sap wood on the outside of the bow as there is red wood on the inside. Otherwise, the bow will get crooked after a while."

Grizzly sneered, "You don't have to tell me how to make a bow! Besides, this is a northern type of bow, and I am going to glue strips of deer sinew on the outside."

"Bah! you and your northern bows. Down south we make good strong bows, and no sinews—round bows for strong men, not flat, flexible bows for women and children and old men like you."

"I am no older than you are, since we are twins!"

Bear said, "YOU MUST be older than I am, since I call you elder brother."

"That doesn't prove anything. You have to call me either elder brother or younger brother. I don't know why you choose to call me elder brother—for all I know, you are the one who came first."

"No, I AM NOT!" roared Bear, exasperated. "You came first because I call you elder brother, and that PROVES it!"

Grizzly turned to Antelope and said; "My brother is bright, no?"

Antelope answered, "He thinks it's poison oak, Coyote thinks it's the HA-HAS, but I will tell you what it is; it's the ARGUING SICKNESS. And you, Grizzly brother-in-law, will soon catch it if you don't watch out."

Grizzly took up again the stave he was shaping for a bow. He said, "We are going to need some sinew, some deer sinew to glue on the back of the bow, and also to make bowstrings. Sister-in-law, did you save the sinew from the back of that deer we killed back there?"

"Of course, I did. What do you take me for, a nitwit? A careful housewife always saves the sinew." She rummaged in her pack and brought out the sinew. It was in two long pieces. She started to shred it, and the children helped her.

Coyote said, "I'll prepare the glue." He pounded deer hooves and fish bones and pieces of pine gum together on a flat slab of rock until it was like a fine powder, then he heated water in a small basket by dropping in hot rocks. He put the powder in it and stirred and stirred.

When the sinew was all shredded they chewed and chewed it, then they laid the glue, a thin layer of it, on the back of the bow, and then they laid the pieces of the shredded sinew on top of the glue, very carefully. Then they put the bow on top of a rock for the glue to dry.

"You must put the sinew on very, very slowly," Grizzly said.

Bear paid no attention to them. He was not getting better very fast, he kept wandering around the camp, sitting one place and then getting up to sit down somewhere else. Antelope said to him, "You'll never get well that way. You are restless, you worry too much. WHAT ARE YOU worrying about?"

"We ought to be moving on!" said Bear. "Here we are in camp, eating all our provisions."

"Oh, STOP worrying. We have lots of provisions yet, and when they are gone, we'll go hunting again and fishing and root-digging. It's time for paha roots to be just right and sweet and juicy, and the laurel nuts. WHAT'S the matter with you, man? You just worry, worry all the time. That's what's the matter with you. That's why you are sick!!!"

"Maybe you are right," Bear said, "but I don't feel well."

Oriole Girl had been listening to them. She said, "Why don't you get a doctor? Isn't Grandfather Coyote a doctor?"

"Of course he is, but he won't admit it, won't take the trouble."

"What trouble would it be to him?"

"Ha, you don't know, little girl, but it's very dangerous work to be a doctor. You have to keep in touch with your medicine, and your medicine may turn against you if you are not careful. If you don't keep him tame all the time. Coyote Old Man wants peace; he is not looking for trouble."

"Oh, I see," Oriole said thoughtfully. Then she added, "I know a woman, a Loon Woman. I saw her fishing up there, up the stream where there is a beaver pond, and I talked to her, and she looked as if she was one of the kind you talk about, a doctor. Maybe she would help us."

Antelope said, "What were you doing up there?"

"Oh, looking for berries. She is the one who gave me the fish."

"Well, go up there again and see if she will help us. But look out for those Beaver people, they are water people and they don't like land people like us, or people from the air, like you."

"Oh, I know," said Oriole.

She went up the stream. When she arrived at the beaver pond the Beaver boys were playing water polo.

"There is our land person!" they cried. "Come on, land girl, come and play with us. We'll teach you to swim."

"No, I haven't come to play with you. Where is that woman Loon who was fishing here the other day?"

"Your friend, the witch? We killed her and we'll kill you too."

"I'm not afraid of you," Oriole said. "I have a powerful medicine to protect me. Do you think I would have come here alone if I didn't have a strong medicine hidden in my skirt? I dare you to come and bother me."

The Beaver boys were talking among themselves. They were saying, "Maybe she is telling the truth. Maybe we'd better leave her alone. These land people are bad people."

Oriole went along the shore of the lake until the Beaver boys couldn't see her, then she took out her string of abalone pearls and dropped them into the water. The necklace looked like a beautiful watersnake under the water. It started to wriggle and swim along the shore, in and out between clumps of tules and reeds. Oriole followed along the shore, and around a bend she found the Loon Woman. The Loon was fishing. She saw the necklace swimming toward her and she picked it up.

"You must be in trouble again, child. How did you find me here, fishing on this lonely lake? Weren't you afraid?"

"No, because these beads protected me, beautiful Loon. Yes, I am in trouble. My uncle is sick down below in our camp, and I have come to ask you to doctor him."

"I am not a doctor," said Loon, "I am only a woman who fishes and minds her own business."

"Oh yes, beautiful Loon, I think you are a doctor. Please come and help my uncle who is sick. My grandfather has plenty of beads in his sack. I am sure he will give you some."

"Has he those beads that they make from rocks they find in the earth down south; those which turn pink when they are heated in the fire? They are very beautiful and rare. I have only a few of them. We do not have that kind here. Does your grandfather have that kind in his little sack?"

"I don't know. It is a very little sack that he carries around his neck, but I have seen him pull a lot of things out of it. I don't know how he does it."

"Oooh," said the Loon, "I think I have heard of him before. I'll go tomorrow and see if I can help you. Now, go back to your camp. I must finish my fishing. Take this string of fish with you and give it to your people."

Oriole went back. She passed the place where the Beaver boys were playing water polo and she made a face at them.

"Well," they cried, "did you find your friend the witch?"

"No, she was dead, but I found her bones and I spoke to them and they said for me to go back and if I saw you boys to tell you to get ready because these bones are coming to borrow some acorn flour from you. You hear? Her bones will be here very soon."

The Beaver boys were uneasy. One of them said, "I don't like that kind of talk. I am going home." He dived under the water and disappeared—and all the other boys dived and disappeared.

When Oriole got home, Fox Boy said, "I see you found your fish tree again."

Oriole didn't pay any attention, she went to the grown-ups and said, "I found the Loon Woman and she promised she would be here tomorrow."

It was still early when Oriole got back to camp. Antelope said, "I can see that we are going to be here two or three days or more. Why don't we move camp over there to that clump of redwoods? It's too hot here in the sun, it would be cooler over there."

For there was a circle of redwoods not far from where they were camped, one of those circles caused by the falling of giant trees. Such a tree, when it finally dies of old age, falls and all around where the old man stood a new generation springs up from the roots of the old one. At first many saplings push up quickly, crowding one another, and at last only the strongest survive in a circle. They themselves grow old, centuries old—but what is a century to a redwood tree?

So they moved their camp and that evening Coyote Old Man said an especially good night to their new hosts. "Good night, Redwoods. Protect us in our sleep. We are good people, traveling on our way to the coast. We have no quarrel with anyone, we wish harm to no one. Good night."

In the middle of the night the wind rose, a gentle wind from the uplands, a warm wind, sweeping down the canyons. Oriole nudged Fox under the rabbit-skin blanket and whispered into his ear, "Listen, can you hear someone singing?"

The next morning at breakfast Fox Boy asked, "Do redwood trees have to sing for their shadows in the dawn?"

Bear answered, "I don't know. How is it, Coyote?"

"I don't know either; I don't even know whether they have shadows."

Fox was shocked.

"Why, Grandfather, I thought you knew everything."

"Of course, I don't, silly. Nobody knows everything."

Fox thought for a while, then he said, "Not even Kuksu?"

Coyote replied, "I don't know about Kuksu. He is one that no one knows much about. When Marumda wanted to make the world he went and asked the Kuksu how to do it. I don't know whether the Kuksu knows everything or not. You will have to ask him yourself—IF you see him."

"But when will I see him?"

"I told you before, maybe you will never see him. Only a few people have ever seen him, always in lonely places, thinking and studying. And when you ask him anything, he never answers. He merely squints and smiles and disappears."

The Loon Woman arrived about the middle of the day. She had brought several fish for a present and these she gave to Antelope. Then she looked at Bear, who was feeling miserable. She never spoke to him,

merely looked intently at him, then she took Oriole by the hand and said, "Let's go pick berries."

"But aren't you going to doctor my uncle?"

"Yes, surely, but not until night sets in. We doctors never work during the day, only after dark, after the sun sets. Come, let's go and pick berries."

When they were away from the camp Loon said to Oriole, "Who is that old man in the camp?"

"That's Old Man Coyote. My father says he is a doctor but won't admit it."

"Most likely. Doctors seldom admit it, especially when they are getting old. It's too much trouble—too dangerous. I thought he was a doctor from the way he was watching me. Doctors are always watching other doctors."

Oriole asked, "Why do they?"

"Because a doctor is always afraid that another doctor will steal his medicine, his *damaagomi,* away from him."

"Oh, I see. Who is your medicine, Doctor Loon?"

"He is the Big Lizard. They call him *wa'wa lunneq.*"

"Oh, I know, the one who lost all his children, the Terrible Lizard, the one who hunts on Mount Shasta. He lost all his children and it made him glum and fierce. I have heard my father tell stories about him."

Loon laughed.

"Yes, that's the one, and he surely is fierce, but I have him pretty well tamed. Child, would you be afraid of him if I asked you to be my helper when I doctor your uncle tonight?"

Oriole replied, "No, beautiful Loon, I would never

be afraid with you near me. But how can I help you? I don't know anything about doctoring."

"You don't have to know anything, all you have to do is to repeat what the doctor says—just repeat his words—because, you see, when my medicine arrives in the air and is floating over my head, and I start to question him, I will be the only one who can hear him. I will repeat everything he says in a loud voice, but I will be so excited that I will be out of my head. When I come out of my trance I will remember nothing and I will have to be told what I said."

"But, Doctor Loon, I still don't see why you need me to repeat what you say, since everybody else there will hear it as well as I."

The Loon smiled.

"Child, you want to know everything, don't you? Very well, I will tell you. My medicine, that Terrible Lizard, is dangerous. I am not afraid of him and yet I am. I need someone near me whom I love and trust, to give me courage."

Oriole blushed and said, "Oh, I see. Yes, I am ready to help you, elder sister, and I will not be afraid."

Loon Woman was pensive for a moment, then she said, "Yes, it is dangerous to be a doctor. Some doctors are fool enough to get trickery mixed up in it, but they always have to pay for it later on. It confuses the doctor's medicine, his *damaagomi,* the *damaagomi* gets wilder and wilder, and in the end he turns against his father or mother the doctor, and destroys him. No, it is hard to be a doctor, and I would rather not be one, but you helped my grandmother when she was stranded on a rock in the lake and now I will help to cure your uncle for you."

Now they went back to the camp. Antelope was weaving her basket. Loon Woman watched the weaving in silence for a while, then she said, "You weave well. What pattern is that?"

"It's the quail pattern. Do you also weave, Doctor Loon?"

"Oh, I weave fishing nets, fishing baskets, fish traps, you know, rough stuff, nothing pretty like this work you do. I am only a fishing person."

They sat talking together. Grizzly was gluing more strips of sinew onto the back of the bow and Fox was helping him. Grizzly spoke. "Do you know the country to the west of here, Doctor Loon?"

"Yes, for a way. Not far from here you will come to a high ridge. On the other side of the ridge you will have to cross a wide valley, the valley of the Grass people. These Grass people are strange people, they are always bowing to each other. When the wind changes they fight each other, but they are not dangerous to strangers unless you should start a fire. Fires are strictly forbidden in their country. Then you will go over another high ridge and come to the valley of the Fire people. They and the Grass people are sworn enemies. These people are dangerous when they are angry, but they won't bother strangers unless they bring in contraband water. They have a horror of water in any form and they are very strict about it.

"After the next ridge you will enter the land of the Water people. I don't need to tell you that they and the Fire people are sworn enemies, but you won't have any trouble, although you will find them a somewhat mournful lot. They and the Grass people are great friends and would like to visit each other, but the Fire people stand between them and won't let them cross Fire territory. After that you won't have any more trouble on your way north."

After supper, when dusk arrived, Loon said to Oriole, "Now, my helper, you go out to the edge of the brush facing the north and call several times for my medicine. *Ittu, damaagomi, tunnoo ittu damaagomi tunnoo.*"

Oriole did so, then came back and sat down on the ground next to Loon. The others were sitting around the fire in a circle. Then Loon started her song. At first she was merely humming the song, then gradually she sang louder and louder.

A no lano lano laz nez . . .

All the others joined in, one by one: Bear, Grizzly, Antelope, Fox, even Coyote Old Man. They all sang the song in unison. When they were in full swing, Loon quit singing; she had closed her eyes and seemed to be asleep. Suddenly she clapped her hands, and everybody stopped singing. The silence was oppressive, then there was a whirr in the darkness over their heads, something like the noise made by a nighthawk swooping.

Loon cried, "Ha! you have been a long time coming. I have been calling and calling you."

Oriole repeated it word for word, then, even before Oriole had quite finished, Loon cried again, "My mother, I was hunting on Mount Shasta. I came as soon as I heard you."

Then Loon cried, "Why did you call me? I was hunting. Why did you bother me?"

Oriole was repeating, word for word.

Loon cried, "Hold your tongue or I will whip you. There is a sick man here and I want you to find out what is the matter with him."

"How do I know what is the matter with him, and what do I care? I want to go back to my hunting."

"If you don't do as I order you, I will break your bow, I will break your spear, I will blind your children in the land of the dead."

"My mother, my mother, don't do that! I will obey you, I will obey you. I will go, I will go!"

"Go then. Hunt around for the trouble. Hunt well or you know what I will do."

Then Loon was silent, she seemed to be sleeping except that every little while she was shaken by a spasm of trembling. Then she began to moan. Everybody around the fire was silent.

Then once more she started to sing and everyone joined her. Once more she clapped her hands and all were silent. Again there was the whirr in the darkness overhead. Loon cried, "My mother, my mother, here I am. I have found something. That man has lost his shadow. There is a whirligig beetle not far from here who has something to do with it. That is all I could find out. Now let me go back to my hunting."

Loon stopped speaking. She seemed to be asleep again then she hiccoughed several times and began to shake violently. All at once she gave a weird cry and fainted away.

Old Man Coyote said, "Don't touch her, don't move her. Cover her with a rabbit-skin blanket and let her sleep until morning. She is a good doctor. I have heard of her but I have never seen her work. You will be all right now, Bear."

"I don't know," grumbled Bear. "I don't see how she helped me."

Antelope exclaimed, "You heard yourself what her medicine said, that you had lost your shadow. That's what has been the trouble with you."

"Yes, but how is it going to help me to know that? I can't live without my shadow."

Grizzly said, "Think a bit, Brother, although that may be hard for you. Her medicine said something about a whirligig beetle having something to do with it."

Bear thought for a while then he exclaimed, "Oh, I wonder!"

"What is it you wonder? Speak up, man," said Antelope.

"That day when I was taken sick you remember I went root-digging with brother Grizzly by the banks of the stream. Well, when I was bending over to dig up some water lilies I remember I saw a whirligig beetle whirling around in the water. It amused me to see him whirling around and around like that and I laughed. But I didn't do anything to him. I stayed there looking at him so long that when I straightened up I felt kind of dizzy. That's all about the whirligig. I don't see what he has to do with my losing my shadow."

Antelope said, "My, but that man of mine is stupid sometimes. Of course, that's where your shadow went. The whirligig stole it."

"How could he steal my shadow?"

Even Fox Boy laughed.

"Haven't you ever seen your shadow in a pool of water? The whirligig only had to grab it."

But Bear still insisted, "Why should he want to steal my shadow? I didn't do anything to him, I just laughed because he looked so funny whirling around like a crazy man."

"Really, my man, you are impossible," Antelope said. "How would you like it if a stranger came to your camp and stared and stared at you and then started to hold his sides with laughter."

"Well, maybe, maybe. But how am I going to get back my shadow? I can't live without it, you know."

"Oh, don't keep repeating that. We will find a way. We will ask Doctor Loon tomorrow."

"You will be all right," said Coyote.

"Well, maybe," Bear grumbled.

During the night the children heard the night wind blowing gently—at least Oriole heard it, and she nudged Fox Boy sleeping by her side under the rabbit-skin blanket.

"Listen, but don't forget yourself and talk." They both listened. One of the redwood trees was speaking.

"Well, did you hear what the Loon doctor said about a whirligig beetle stealing that man's shadow?"

Another tree spoke.

"You always get things mixed up. It wasn't the Loon doctor who said that, it was her *damaagomi,* her medi-

99

cine, the Terrible Lizard, the one who has lost all his children."

"I know, I know, you don't have to tell me, but what puzzles me is how did the Terrible Lizard find out?"

"Because he is a spirit-man, you stupid. He is a supernatural being. He went around here and there asking questions or maybe just listening to people talking. Maybe some of the whirligig people were talking about it among themselves and they didn't know he was listening. They didn't see him—you can't see those supernatural beings unless they are willing to let you see them."

"I know that," said the first redwood. "You don't have to tell me."

"Then why do you ask such foolish questions?"

Fox Boy could not help himself; he burst out laughing in spite of Oriole who was pushing his head under the blanket. The redwood trees were silent and the night wind died down.

The Hoot Owl was hunting and calling his mate. When she came, he said, "Have you heard the news? It was whirligig beetle who stole that sick man's shadow. I just heard the redwood trees talking about it."

The Hoot Owl's mate said, "Oh, I must hurry and tell Mrs. Nighthawk about it. She will be very much interested," and she hurried off on silent wings.

When morning came Bear felt better, but Loon Woman was still dizzy; she could not remember anything about the night before, and they had to repeat to her everything that was said during her trance. Then she thought and thought for a long time. At last she said to Bear, "Can you remember the place where you saw that whirligig?"

"Oh yes, sure."

"Then go there again and sing this song. It's the whirligig song."

Whirligig Song

Loon sang it two or three times, then asked Bear, "Do you think you can remember it?"

"Sure. Listen."

Antelope said, "He may not be very good at thinking, but he is a first class singer."

Loon said, "Go, then, to that place where you saw the whirligig and sing his song. He will soon come to the surface to see who is calling him. Then is the time for you to speak to him and ask him to give you back your shadow. You might say to him firmly, 'Mr. Whirligig, please give me back my shadow. You should do it, because Doctor Loon has Terrible Lizard for a hunting dog.' That's all you will say to him. Don't try to explain. Don't argue. Just turn around and come straight back without ever turning your head, not even if he calls you."

"All right, I will do just what you have told me."

Bear started to the stream. As he went up the bank, Antelope called after him, "AND REMEMBER, DON'T ARGUE!"

While Bear was away recovering his shadow the rest busied themselves around the camp. Loon Woman and Antelope sat together and talked. Loon took up the baby Quail and sang a song to her. The children were helping Grizzly to glue more and more sinews on the back of the bow. It was a very flexible bow, and as the sinews and glue dried, their shrinking was already pulling the bow into a backward curve. Coyote Old

Man was making a bow-string, chewing sinews just enough to make them soft and pliable and then twisting them against his thigh.

Presently they heard Bear coming back downstream, lustily singing the whirligig song.

"Listen to him," Grizzly said. "I guess he got his shadow back, all right."

The next morning the Bear party started early and followed the directions the Loon Woman had given them. After a long climb they arrived at the summit of a ridge. Down below they saw a wide valley—the land of the Grass people. There were multitudes of them, thousands upon thousands.

"Goodness," cried Fox. "I didn't think there were so many people in the whole world and here they are, all packed in one valley!"

These were strange people, these Grass people. When the wind blew they went into a wild dance with much bowing and curtseying to each other. The dance grew more and more frenzied, the Grasses fought and stabbed and clubbed each other with fury, then when the wind abated, they resumed their normal occupations after a few more polite bowings to each other. There did not seem to be any dead or wounded.

The Bear party descended into the valley gradually. Soon they began to meet with groups of Grass people, tall fellows, some of them armed with bows-and-arrows and others with spears and daggers. But all of them were thin—very, very thin. That was the reason they never were hurt in their frenzied dances when the wind blew down the valley: the arrows, spears, and daggers never found their bodies.

Finally the Bear party reached the floor of the valley. Just as they were going to pay their respects to the Grass Chief, the wind started to blow, at first gently; and all the Grass people began to dance and sing and curtsey to each other. Fox and Oriole could not resist it, so they started swaying and bowing and curtseying to each other. Then Antelope caught it and she started swaying and curtseying to Bear and Grizzly. At that moment the Chief of the Grass people arrived, bowing and swaying and curtseying right and left. And now Coyote Old Man was swaying and curtseying to the Grass Chief.

Now the Grass Chief made a speech of welcome:

"We are happy to see you go through our land, very happy indeed. But please do not build any campfires. We have a horror of fire, it reminds us too much of our traditional enemies, the Fire people, who live in the next valley. They are horrible people, quarrelsome, violent, treacherous. Indeed, I grieve to think you have to cross their land. Watch out for them. But after you are through their land, if they have not killed and burned you, you will arrive at the land of the Water people. Ah! they are wonderful people, generous and kind. But we so seldom see them. The dreadful Fire people are afraid of the Waters and won't let them go through the Fire valley. And the Waters, also, are not very brave, I must admit; kind people, generous people, but somewhat indolent and long on suffering. Well, go on your way, go on your way, and good luck to you. But please do not make any campfires."

Now a gentle breeze swept down the valley and the Chief and all the Grass people started swaying and bowing gracefully. The Bears could do no less than return the compliment, so they started bowing and swaying to the right and the left and commenced to climb out of the valley.

They started traveling again the next day, *tras . . . tras . . . tras. . . .* They crossed the valley of the Fire people and the valley of the Water people, and early one afternoon when the sun was halfway down, they arrived at a fairly wide stream, you might call it a river. It meandered through the plain and flowed slowly between banks covered with tules and reeds. They decided to camp there for the night.

The next morning they got up early and all went to take a plunge in the river before breakfast. Oriole could not swim, but Fox Boy had been raised on the shore of a large lake and he was a fine swimmer. Now he started to teach Oriole.

At breakfast Antelope said, "We have had pretty hard traveling in the last few days, what with crossing the valleys of those crazy people, Grass and Fire, and those eternally weeping Water people (and I think they were drunk most of the time, too, if you ask me. They drank too much of that water). Anyhow, I am tired and I would like to rest!"

Grizzly said, "Yes, and my moccasins are almost worn out. There are lots of tules here. We can stop and make moccasins for all of us."

Bear said, "Maybe there is arrow wood growing around here. I'll be making arrows. My son has lost nearly all of mine."

"The ones with flint arrowheads?" Antelope asked. "Now, I wouldn't let him have those. Straight-pointed arrows are good enough for rabbits."

Fox said, "I'll go and find you some arrow wood."

"How are you going to find it? Do you know what kind of bushes are good for arrow wood?"

"Of course I know. And I hear old Badger chopping wood over there. I'll go and ask him if there is any arrow wood growing around here. All Badgers are good woodsmen."

Antelope asked, "How do you know that?"

"Oh, I know that much. Come on, Oriole. It's your turn to carry the doctor's cane today." And they went skipping in the direction of the Badger's camp.

Bear said, "That Badger is up mighty early, chopping wood. Why does he need so much wood?"

Grizzly laughed.

"To dry you up over the smoke-hole like Erihutiki, Brother. You are pretty big, you know, and it will take a lot of wood for your carcass."

Antelope burst out with her silver laugh. Bear grumbled, "Woman, you laugh easily. I don't see anything funny in what he said."

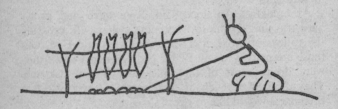

The next day they stayed in camp—the same camp, because Grizzly and Bear had fished in the river and they had caught so many fish that they decided to smoke them. They made a platform of sticks and green twigs, like a grill, with a slow fire underneath, burning all day, and at the same time the sun was shining. On this grill they laid the fish, after they had opened them with obsidian knives, and then they turned them over and over while they were drying.

Next morning a party of antelopes came out of the tules, following the trail in single file—five men and two women and several children. The men and women were very tall and they walked with an elastic step and took long strides. The women wore short buckskin shirts instead of hula skirts of grass, and they wore their hair in two long tresses. The men coiled their hair into a top-knot with a wooden hairpin to hold it.

There was a big log lying athwart the trail, but when they came to it the Antelopes, instead of crawling or dragging themselves over, just leaped over it with the greatest of ease. They were as lithe as wildcats.

They came up to the camp and said, "Hoh," and then sat down quietly, but they were looking curiously at Antelope, and she was looking at them with the same curiosity, for although it isn't good manners for strangers to pay attention to each other at the first meeting, both sides were equally struck with the resemblance between Antelope and these people.

Finally, one of the Antelope men said to the others, speaking in his own language, "That woman over there looks like one of us." (*"Kan snawats slepopka nat neimmi."*)

Then Antelope herself spoke, "I understand what you just said, although I almost never speak that language any longer unless it be with my brother, for there are very few of us left where I live. Where do you come from and where are you going? As for me, I came from the country to the south of here, and these are my people. We are traveling toward the west to visit some relatives who live near the ocean."

One of the Antelope men answered, "Our home is very far from here in the uplands and deserts of the northeast country. We people are wanderers and nomads. We like to wander about where there is plenty of space and a free sky. We don't like the country of mountains and forests."

Antelope translated this speech to Bear and Grizzly. Meanwhile, the children, Fox and Oriole, had made friends with the Antelope children, and soon they were all playing together. The Antelope children had throwing-sticks, and these they threw with much the same motion as spears. Fox and Oriole were soon throwing these sticks with ease.

Bear said, "It's strange; their children know our language but their parents don't." One of the Antelope people then spoke in Bear's tongue, although with some difficulty, "Yes, we do, a little. But children learn much faster than grown-ups."

So the Bear party didn't get started that day. The Antelope people were glad to stop and rest and talk with the others. And the children were having a good time playing together.

The next morning, the Antelopes went to get some rabbits for breakfast. They took with them their throwing sticks which were flat or curved or crooked, and all went out, men, women, and children. At first they went silently through the brush, one by one, each in a different direction, but all starting from one place which was clear of brush. Then, when they were a distance away, and apart from each other, they began to shout and beat the brush, coming back toward the place from which they started. Thus they flushed a number of rabbits. It was a fine sight to see them throwing their curved sticks. They bent way back and then brought the stick forward in one sweeping motion while they jumped forward onto the other foot, so that at the end they sometimes sprawled forward with the throwing arm fully extended. The stick went whirling through the air like a sickle, not far from the ground. They got half a dozen rabbits that way.

Grizzly and Bear had been watching. Grizzly said, "I wouldn't like one of those sticks to hit me, Brother. It might break my leg."

"Not if it hit you in the head! That would break the stick."

"Oh, please," Grizzly said, "don't try joking before breakfast!"

After breakfast everybody started to pack. Then Bear asked the Antelope people, "Why don't you join our party? It won't take you so very far out of your way."

Sunset Tracks, the one who seemed to act as leader, answered, "That's not a bad idea. For my part I am willing, but I don't know what the others will think about it." Then each one of the Antelope men and women spoke in turn, and each agreed to go along with the Bear party.

Fox Boy had made special friends with the boy who seemed to be the leader of the Antelope children. His name was Wahoomi, meaning "he who runs in the tules." Fox Boy had quite a bit of trouble in pronouncing it; he said *"wahommi,"* and the Antelope children laughed. "You said 'he is the wind in the tules.' *Wahoomi* and *wahommi,* they are two different words. One means 'the wind is blowing' and the other means 'he runs.' But it doesn't matter," the Antelope boy said. "Flying like the wind in the tules is just as good as running in the tules." So after that he was called indifferently "Tule-runner" or "Tule-flyer."

Now they came to a stream and there were many tule reeds growing along the bank. Bear said, "Here is a fine place to make camp and weave some tule slippers for the girls. We don't want to have people with tender feet on the trail." So they stopped and made camp.

Somebody was chopping wood somewhere near, *TUL ... TUL ... TUL ... TUL. ...*

Fox said, "I bet it's another old man Badger."

The boy Tule-runner said, "No, it's an old man Porcupine. I can tell by the sound. Listen. He is high up in a tree, chopping wood. Badgers don't climb trees, but Porcupines do. Aren't there Porcupines in your country?"

Fox said, "We have porcupine-tail combs. That's all I know. But I never knew porcupines were people. Do they have tails also?"

"Sure, but it's not a nice furry one like yours. His tail is covered with spikes. Well, you know what they are like since you say you have seen them used for combs."

"Ooh, that's what they are!"

"Yes, and that's what Porcupine fights with, if you bother him. He puts down his head and he hurls that tail of his around, and if it hits you, I tell you, you'll be sorry. Those spikes break, and you can't dig 'em out. They'll stay under your skin forever and drive you crazy. Not many people ever bother with Mister Porcupine!"

"Will you gamble with him?"

"No, indeed! He's too clever! Some people think he is stupid, but I tell you he is not stupid at all."

So the whole party came up to Porcupine's place, and indeed, there he was, high up in a tree, chopping off a limb. Bear called, "Hey, up there, Mister Chief Porcupine, may we camp around here?"

"Certainly, certainly. I'll come down right now and help you make camp. Glad to have visitors."

The children were astonished to see how he came down, digging his long fingernails into the bark of the tree. And they were still more astonished when they saw him amble over to them when he reached the ground. He was short and thickset and bow-legged, and his head, neck, and back were covered with long coarse hair.

This old man Porcupine was very jolly. He recognized Old Man Coyote right away.

"Well, well, well! here is old Grandfather Bupuuga: What are you doing up here?"

"Oh, these people came to my place and woke me up, and made me come along with them."

The old Porcupine then went into his house and returned with a basketful of pine nuts and another of acorn flour, and in no time at all, they had supper ready. After supper as they sat around the fire, Porcupine was admiring the moccasins on the feet of the Antelope girls and he said, "Those moccasins remind me of the story about a great-grandfather of mine and a great-grandfather of yours, Doctor Coyote."

"Oh, an old-time story!" cried the children. "Good! Please tell us the story!"

"All right," said Porcupine.

This coyote had come from way up north, and he had never seen slippers made of tule reeds. Well, one day he went out to gather firewood. There was fresh snow on the ground, and he saw some tracks on the snow. "What beautiful tracks!" he thought. "I wonder what made those tracks." So he followed them, and he arrived at the house of Porcupine. He went in. Porcupine was pounding and grinding nuts. Coyote asked, "Was it you who went by there?"

"Yes, it was. I was gathering firewood."

"Give me some pine nuts," said Coyote.

"All right!" and he gave him a basketful. Coyote soon gobbled them all up.

Then he said, "Where are those fine shoes you were wearing?"

Porcupine smiled. He picked up the tule-reed slippers and threw them over to Coyote. "Here they are! Aren't they nice?"

"Are these the shoes?" said Coyote.

"Certainly! They are the only ones I've got!"

Coyote looked at them. "Let's trade shoes!" he said.

"All right!" said Porcupine.

So Coyote took off his moccasins and put the tule slippers on his feet. Porcupine took Coyote's moccasins and put them away.

"Well, I have to go home and gather firewood," said Coyote. And he started for his place on the run. Soon he stopped and traced back his own steps. "Beautiful tracks!" he said to himself. "I surely got the best of the trade!" And he started again like a streak. He just laid out his tail!! . . . But he had only gone a little way when he stopped again. His feet were hurting him. He didn't know that you had to wear moss inside tule slippers. And now his feet were chafed. He traced back his steps. He saw his tracks were bloody . . . He went back to Porcupine's house. He went in and sat down. "These shoes are no good!" he said. "I want to trade them back!" Porcupine didn't pay any attention to him. "Listen!" said Coyote. "I am hurt. . . . I want to trade them back!" Porcupine didn't pay any attention. Coyote said, "If you don't want to trade them back, then let's run a race for them!" Porcupine didn't pay any attention. Coyote said, "I'll throw in my tump-line as a side bet, and you throw in some pine nuts, and we'll have a race."

But Porcupine said, "No . . . I am satisfied with the trade." But at the same time he was thinking to himself, "I am a mean one, I am a medicine-man!" he was thinking to himself, then: "All right!" he said, "I'll race you."

So they put down their bets. "Listen," said Coyote, "hadn't I better give you a handicap?"

"Never mind," said Porcupine, and he started. He ambled along; qooobin, qoobin, qooobin. . . .

"Run! . . ." yelled Coyote. Porcupine kept on ambling along: qooobin . . . qoobin . . . qooobin. . . . "I'll beat him easy if he doesn't go any faster than that! . . ." thought Coyote, and he drew in his belt. He started to run and he caught up with Porcupine in a few jumps. "He is no good! . . ." he thought to himself. He sat down to give him a handicap again. He caught up with him once more. "Run faster this time!" he cried. "Here we are together again!" Again he gave him a handicap and again he caught up with him.

Then they stopped and talked. "Now, try again," said Coyote, and Porcupine started once more, but Coyote lay down to take a nap, and Porcupine went on ambling along, *qoobin . . . qoobin . . . qoobin. . . .*

And as he went along, Porcupine thought, "Let there be plums!" Thus he thought because he was a medicine-man, Porcupine was. And he thought, "Let there also be cherries! Let there be crickets. . . . That will do, *kistam-yumi*." He had power, the Porcupine. Then he started again to amble as fast as he could. Then he also made a cloud to come by his power, and then he ran home to his winter house close by. He went in and sat down. "Pheeewwww . . ." he blew out his breath. "I think I beat him," he thought. . . .

So Porcupine had gone back to his house. Now Coyote got up from his nap, yawned, and thought, "I'd better start running again and catch up with that Porcupine . . . but that's all right, I am a running-man, I am a fast runner, I am!" and he went off in a run. He ran and ran, but he lost his bearings in the fog and he was going round and round a pine tree. He thought, "Is he home already, I wonder? He might beat me yet!" He ran into a patch of sagebrush and there he saw some ripe cherries on the bushes. He stopped and ate and filled himself.

Then he started to run again but he saw some plums all ripe on the bushes, and he couldn't help stopping and eating them till his belly was full. He started to run again, and now he saw a lot of crickets hopping around. He started to chase them and eat them one by one as he caught them. Then he wondered again about Porcupine. "I wonder if he might beat me. . . ." He started to run again and came to the rim of a cliff. It was full of fog below the rim of the cliff: Porcupine had made it come by his power. Coyote was running at top speed. . . .

His Big Maggot in his head warned him: "U! U! U! Look out," because Coyote kept maggots inside his head for pets. So the oldest Maggot warned him, but

Coyote couldn't stop. He went rolling and rolling over and over down the cliff.

He yelled, "My Big Maggot, what shall I do?!"

His Big Maggot answered, "That's not the way to run a race, stopping along to eat your belly full!"

Coyote cried: "My middle Maggot, what shall I do? Help me! Help me quick!"

His middle Maggot said, "What can I do? I can't help it!"

Coyote cried, "Oh, that's what you always say. . . . My LITTLE Maggot, tell me what to do!"

"Turn on your side and dig in your toes and climb down the cliff."

Coyote climbed down slowly and when he reached the bottom he lit out again for Porcupine's house. He got there and walked up the roof to the smoke-hole and went down the ladder. *"Tsa'a'a'a . . ."* he thought. I am going to murder him! I'll kill him and then I'll eat him!" he thought as he was going down the center-post ladder. . . . But when he got down he couldn't find him anywhere in the house. So he went out again and went around the house and found Porcupine's tracks and tracked him to a pine tree. There he was up on top, the Porcupine, grinding pine nuts. "Hey, up there, what are you doing up there? Are you moving camp?"

"Oh, the vermin and fleas were too thick in the house, so I moved my camp up here. . . . But I beat you in the race. . . . What were you going to do? I waited for you a long time and then I moved my camp up here."

"Well . . . I saw you running not far away, and then I saw some plums and cherries and crickets and I stopped to eat them."

"That's not a good way to run a race. . . . When two men run a race they usually run along together."

Coyote said, "Well . . . I'm hungry, give me some pine nuts to eat!"

Porcupine said, "Of course I beat you! That was last

winter when there was snow on the ground, and now it's autumn and the cherries and plums are ripe, you say. Did you expect me to wait for you forever?"

"I am hungry, I tell you!" said Coyote. "Give me some pine nuts to eat!"

Porcupine said, "I beat you, that's what I did to you," and he paid no more attention to him.

Coyote growled, "All right, I'll kill you yet, you'll see!!"

He went and looked for some firewood and brought it back to the foot of the pine tree and set fire to it. But Porcupine stayed aloft all night. Dawn came and Coyote was very sleepy. He thought, "Bah! Come daylight and the tree will fall down," and he poked the fire. Porcupine was wondering, "Is he watching me?" Coyote started to snore. Then Porcupine came down. He took down with him some of his provisions and hid them among the rocks. Then he climbed up the tree again and got down the rest of his provisions and hid them in the rocks around the place.

The tree fell over. Coyote jumped up in his fright. Then he ran to the head of the tree, but he didn't see Porcupine there. He ran around the tree: no Porcupine! He went back to the burning stump, and from there he tracked him, and tracked him, and tracked him and finally found him in a hole in the rocks. There he was grinding pine nuts. "What! Have you moved camp again?" Porcupine didn't pay any attention. "Give me something to eat!" said Coyote. Porcupine didn't pay any attention. "If you don't pay any attention to me, I'll kill you!" said Coyote, "I'll smoke you to death!" Then Coyote brought some wood, piled it up at the mouth of the hole and set fire to it. . . . .

Old man Porcupine was stopping and lighting his pipe. He was smoking for a long time and didn't say anything.

"Well, now, what happened? What was the end of it?" asked Fox. "That isn't any way to end a story! What happened to Mr. Porcupine?"

"What was the end of the story? Well . . . Porcupine made the north wind come by his power and it blew the smoke away. Then Coyote got discouraged and quit!"

The next day they decided to hold a deer drive, since they were so many people gathered together. Sunset Tracks said to the Bears, "You and your people be the shooters, and we will do the driving. We are used to working together and we understand each other's signals."

So everybody took part in the deer drive, men, women, and children. Even the old man Porcupine and Coyote went along. But before they started, the Antelope people sang a hunting song.

Fox Boy asked his friend Wind-in-the-tules if the song meant anything.

"It has something to do with a five-pointer buck, but I don't understand all of it. Let's ask Sunset Tracks. He is my uncle and a great hunter."

Sunset Tracks said, "Yes, the words have to do with a five-pointer buck. They're something like this: 'I wish for a five-pointer to come and meet me.' You don't say that you are going to kill him, you just ask him to come and meet you. He'll come if he wants to.

118

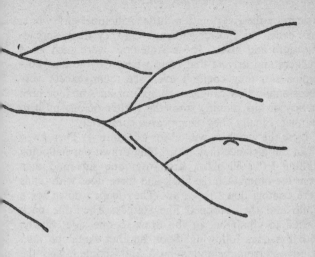

That's where your hunting luck comes in. You can't make a deer come if he doesn't want to, no matter how clever you are. And if you have broken any rules, there is no use asking the deer to come and meet you, you might just as well stay at home. Matter of fact, it would be better to stay at home, because if you go you'll spoil the other fellow's hunting luck. If you have broken any rules, your own power will turn against you and maybe kill you. It will become poison. At least, that's what we say up north in our country."

"Yes, we also say the same thing in my country," said Bear.

And now they started. The two bears, Fox and Oriole hid themselves in the brush on the side of a draw. The deer were bound to pass by that spot when they were driven from behind. The others went up the draw on the other side of the wind. First, old man Porcupine stopped and hid himself in the brush. Old Man Coyote crossed over to the other side of the draw and posted himself. Farther up, two of the women hid, woman

Asleep-by-the-river and a little Antelope girl whom they called the Flower-gatherer. On they went, spreading more and more. These Antelopes were such good trackers and drivers that from where Coyote and Porcupine sat, they couldn't even see them, except very occasionally they caught a glimpse of an Antelope man or boy or girl running from the shelter of one bush to another. Finally, they disappeared completely.

Now the watchers waited for a long time. Then away off in the distance they heard long drawn out hallooing coming from all sides, first from one side and then from the other. A large buck and three does with fauns were coming down the draw. They leaped down for a while and then stopped like statues. Then the buck started to climb out of the draw to one side, slowly, with the does following. Soon another Antelope man stood out from behind a bush and shouted, and the deer all turned and leaped down the draw again.

"Now listen, children," said Grizzly, "don't shoot at the does and fawns, only the buck. And wait until he is quite close; there are four of us and we can't all miss him. But don't get up to shoot. Don't show yourselves. Shoot from lying down, and don't get excited."

And so they shot the buck, all four of them, and none of their arrows missed. Grizzly had a powerful bow and his arrow went deep, and then, as the buck passed him, he stood up and hurled his spear. The spear hit the buck between the ribs. The buck took a few more leaps and lay down. It was a big buck with the velvet shredding from his antlers. Grizzly and Bear packed him home by turns. Soon the Antelopes began to arrive in camp singing the deer song.

It was a mournful tune. Grizzly explained to the children that the Antelopes were sorry for the deer because they had killed him, so they were singing to his shadow to appease him. "Please don't be angry with us, we are hungry. Our people are hungry, so we had to kill you to feed them. Don't be angry with us."

They skinned the buck in no time and split the head open to take out the brain to tan the hide. Fox noticed that the head was full of maggots. He said, "Wow! do all deer have maggots like that in their heads?"

One of the Antelope men said, "Not always, but many of them have. We call these maggots *Hi'wa* in our language."

"Doesn't it bother them?"

"Probably, just like ticks and fleas. But they can't get rid of them."

"What a thing to have in one's head," said Fox.

"I don't know. They say that old Coyote in the stories had three of them in his head. He kept them for pets; a big maggot, a little maggot, and a middle-size maggot. And the Coyote always asked their advice. The big maggot always gave him good advice, but Coyote never listened to him. He would ask the middle maggot, and the middle maggot would say the same thing. 'Oh, you don't know what you are talking about,' Coyote would say. 'My little maggot, you tell me.' Then the little maggot would tell him the opposite of his brothers. Coyote always followed his little maggot's advice and that's how he always got into trouble."

Now they mixed the brains of the buck with some moss and grit and they spread a little of it on the inside of the hide. Then they rolled up the hide into a bundle and wrapped it in wet leaves and put it away to ripen. In a few days the hair would come off easily, and then they would scrape away the grain of the hide, carefully, with stone scrapers, then stretch and stretch and stretch the hide for days. The desert people were known for making beautiful buckskin. Sometimes they would also steep it with certain barks and smoke it very slowly. Then it turned a brown color and was almost waterproof.

And they saved the hooves. Forty or fifty dried hooves, strung on a buckskin fringe, made a rattle that had a nice sound, somewhat like jingle bells. Of course, they saved the sinew for backing bows, and for fine sewing threads. Out of the two forelegs they made awls. The base of the antlers was saved for making chisels, and the whole skin of the head was saved to make a stuffed deer-head decoy.

In a few days they started again, *tras* . . . *tras* . . . *tras* . . . .

The trail wound in and out through slowly rising foothills. There were many outcroppings of rock, jutting out everywhere. Soon the party was strung out in a long straggling line. Coyote Old Man and Antelope were taking their time and bringing up the rear. The Bears were away ahead of them. And way way ahead of the Bears were the Antelope men and women, almost running in their fast elastic stride. This seemed to be the only way they could travel, because they were desert people. At intervals they would sit down and wait patiently for the rest of the party to catch up. They just didn't know how to travel slowly. The Antelope children were the same, and Fox Boy and Oriole Girl had to work to keep up with them, but they were too proud to be left behind.

Grizzly said, "I think when we get to the top of that last ridge we will be able to see the ocean—but we won't get there today. I went through here once, long ago, many years ago. I visited the Crane people. Then they had lots of things; they seemed to be very rich."

"I have heard they have beautiful dances," said Sunset Tracks, "especially one called the White Deer Dance. I am anxious to see that. Our people don't know how to dance. We live in the desert and we are always moving camp and wandering. I guess you have to be settled in villages to have good ceremonies and

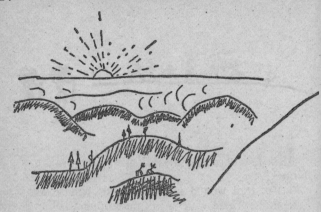

dances. We are good hunters and gamblers, but that's all."

When they started to pack the next morning, Antelope missed the little bundle of quills that the old Porcupine had given her. She looked through her pack and took out everything, but the quills weren't there.

"I must have dropped them when I unpacked last evening," she said. They all looked around the camp but the quills were nowhere to be found.

All the next day they kept climbing and climbing. There were few trees, but very thick brush. At last they reached the top of a high ridge at sunset. The view was magnificent, and far away they could see the ocean shimmering in the light of sunset. They all stood without speaking for a long time, and then they all hurried to make camp before the light failed.

Everybody helped, all except the little Antelope girl, Flower-Gatherer, who seemed listless. She and Oriole had become great friends. Oriole said, "What's the matter? You don't seem happy. Are you sick?"

"Oh, I am just tired, I guess . . . that long climb."

After supper they all began to talk about the Crane people whom they were going to visit.

"Those people don't live in the kind of underground houses we do, or camp around like you Antelopes," Grizzly said. "They have houses made of thick planks of wood. They are great workers in wood, and there is lots of redwood and fir in that country. They have good carving tools, chisels and adzes, and some of them bone, some of stone. When they want to make a boat, they cut down a tree, and little by little, they dig the inside out. They make a little fire and burn some of the trunk, and then carve out the burnt part, and do the same thing over and over again. It may take them a whole year to make a boat. They are great fishermen. They live mostly on fish.

"And they don't have clamshell beads, like ours. For beads they use little tiny sea shells, pinkish-red. These look like a wolf's tooth, and they are hollow. When they have a dance, the men deck themselves out in grand style. Like us, they wear a ring of abalone shell through the nose, and in the ears a leg bone from crane birds, with tufts of feathers at each end. Yes, they are rich people, but they pay too much attention to wealth—they are not open-handed like us. They are proud of their wealth, and they like to show off. But they are good people, just the same. I always got along well with them. Oh, I tell you, they are very different from us! But you ought to see their dances! They take place in the fall of the year. I think it's a little early but I hope we will see some of them, especially the White Deerskin dance."

"What is a white deer?" asked Fox.

"Sometimes, very, very rarely, a deer is born who is pure white all over. They use several of these white deerskins in that dance, the whole skin with the white hair on, and the head too, with the ears and antlers. They attach them to long poles and wave them about, like bucks standing straight on their hind legs. I tell you, it's a beautiful sight to watch in the light of the fires!"

"Oh, I hope we will see that!" said Antelope.

The next day they started the descent from the high ridge, following a stream down a steep canyon. After a while the canyon opened into a beautiful valley. Quite a large river flowed gently through the valley, and there they saw the first villages of the Crane people, also many boats and canoes. The Crane people were very friendly. Antelope made inquiries about her sister. She was told that the sister lived farther downstream where another large river joined this one. There the Bear party would find a large village and many people.

Finally, the party arrived at the village and there was a great reunion between Antelope and her sister, whom she had not seen for many years. Soon Fox, Oriole and the Antelope children were playing with the Crane children. But Oriole in a little while came back to stay with the little Flower-Gatherer, who was sick. The little girl's mother was crying, and everybody felt sad. The little girl was feverish and looked at everyone with haunted eyes.

Antelope said to her sister, "Haven't you any doctors around here?"

"Oh yes, of course we have, and good ones too, but

they want to be paid much money. However, if the sick person is not cured, they must return the money. I'll go and get a strong doctor to come this evening. She is one of our best doctors."

That the doctor should demand to be paid for his services seemed amazing to the desert Antelopes.

"Our doctors never demand money or beads or anything. You give them something if you like because they have helped you, but that's all."

That evening a woman doctor arrived. She wore many feathers in her hair. She sang and danced, but all by herself, she recited many prayers, but she didn't call any power or medicine or poison, like the Loon Woman. It was all a cut and dried ritualistic performance. Bear had seen something like it among his poeple, but not so complicated.

The desert Antelopes were nonplussed; they looked on open-mouthed and didn't understand any of the things that the doctor was doing. Only when she went to the sick child and put her lips to the little girl's chest and started to make a sucking noise, did they recognize anything they understood. The doctor then stood up and took out of her mouth the "pain" she had extracted by sucking. It was a little bit of a thing like a splinter of glass. She showed it to everybody in the dim light of the fire, and then threw it into the fire to destroy it. Then she went home.

But the next day the little girl was sicker than ever. She thrashed about and moaned and seemed out of her head. Everybody was very sad. During the day Oriole went away from camp and wandered by the side of the river. She was thinking, "Oh, if I could call my Doctor Loon!" So she thought to herself as she wandered by the side of the river. She felt very sad for her little sick friend. Then she came to a bend in the river. The water was deep close to the bank, and ran around and around in an eddy. Oriole looked at the water. She looked at the water and said to herself, "I'll try it." Swiftly she took the abalone beads from under her skirt and she dropped them in the water.

Very soon a Salamander Woman came up to the surface. She had a long slim body and her skin was coppery red. The necklace of abalone beads was around her neck. She came out of the water dripping and sat down on the bank. She took off the necklace and handed it to Oriole.

"Here, you dropped your beads. Those are magical beads for water persons. Where did you get them, you a person of the air? You look pretty young for a doctor."

"Oh, I am not a doctor at all. An old Loon Woman gave me those beads because I once helped her, and she told me never to use the beads unless I was in trouble. Now I am in trouble."

"What troubles you, oh person of the air?"

"My friend is sick, and she needs a doctor. But perhaps, you, water person, are a doctor yourself?"

The Salamander Woman smiled.

"Perhaps I am, but if I come and help your sick friend, who will assist me? I have no assistant here, and the people of this place have different ways."

Oriole said, "Maybe I could assist you. Not long

ago I assisted another Loon doctor, when my uncle had lost his shadow."

The Salamander Woman looked at her steadily for a while, then she said, "You talk very differently from the people of this place. They don't even know what a shadow is! Listen. My power is of snakes. Would you be afraid of them?"

"Oh no! That Loon Woman doctor who showed me some things, her power was Lizard."

"Yes, I know," interrupted the Salamander. "The Terrible Lizard, the One-who-has-lost-all-his-children. I know, and I know the Doctor Loon of whom you speak. We doctors know each other everywhere. I will help you. I will come to your camp tomorrow."

Oriole Girl was very happy. She went back to the camp and told her people.

The Salamander Woman arrived the next day in the morning. She acted very much the way the Loon Woman had; she sat a little way apart and didn't seem to pay any attention, then, after a while she motioned to Oriole to come and sit beside her. She said, "Who is that old coyote there?"

"He is my grandfather."

"Is he a doctor?"

"He says he isn't, but we think he is and won't admit it."

"I thought so. He looks like an old doctor, but the old doctors who are really good never admit it. It's too much trouble."

Then the Salamander Woman went to look at the sick girl. The little Flower-Gatherer was very sick and feverish, and mumbling all sorts of wild talk. Salamander looked at her a long time, but didn't speak to her or touch her; then she went and spoke to the other women.

Coyote Old Man was rolling string and paying attention to no one. There were a few of the Crane people, men and women, talking with the Bears and the Antelope men. Once Sunset Tracks went over and joined the women. He didn't seem to be at all surprised to hear them all talking in the Antelope tongue.

He listened for a while and then he said to Salamander Woman, "You seem to know our ways, and if you perform like the doctors in our country, we will be able to help you and sing with you. I don't understand the people here at all. Their ways puzzle me. I don't think much of that doctor they sent yesterday. Maybe she is very good, but it all looked like tomfoolery to us."

When evening came the Salamander Woman acted just like the Loon Doctor. She sent Oriole to the edge of the brush to call her medicine. Then she started her song.

She sang in a very deep voice. All the Antelopes caught the song immediately and sang in unison with her, swaying and shaking their shoulders in the rhythm. None of the Crane people even tried to join in. They had never heard singing of that kind; they didn't know what it was all about. When the Salamander Woman clapped her hands for silence, everybody listened. The frogs and toads by the banks of the river joined the song. Then in the darkness overhead they heard that whirring noise like the swooping of the nighthawk, and with it a rattling noise. Then Salamander cried just the way the Loon had, with Oriole repeating everything she said, trying to imitate her high staccato voice and the way she shouted rapidly without inflections, running her words into each other.

"My mother, I am here! You called me. I heard you. I was sunning myself very far from here, but I heard you and I came. What do you want of me?"

"There is a sick child here, and I want you to help me. But where are the others? Where is Bull Snake? Where is Striped Snake? Where is Green-and-Red Snake? Go and call them. Go. Go!"

Then she sang again and all the Antelopes joined in as before. Some of the Crane people were frightened

and two or three of them slipped away in the darkness.
Once more Salamander clapped her hands for silence,
and now the noise overhead was a din. Salamander
called out again, speaking fast. The sentences came so
quickly, one right after the other, that the words were
jumbled up. Oriole had scarcely time to repeat.

Salamander Woman's voice changed constantly.
Now it was high-pitched and fluty, now it was deep
again. Now it was like a shriek. Oriole Girl was having
a hard time repeating; she couldn't catch all of it. Sunset Tracks came to her aid; he repeated some of the
calls and answers. It was pandemonium.

"Where is Rattlesnake?"

"I am here, Mother. Can't you hear me?"

"I am your Bull Snake, Mother, I am here."

"My Mother, make this little snake here shut up. He
is lying to you."

"I am not lying! I tell you, I was talking to Raven
on top of the Big Mountain. He says there is Porcupine
mixed up in it."

"Oh, go on! What have Porcupines to do with it?"

"Quiet, I tell you. I am not talking to you. I am
talking to our mother."

Then Salamander gave a long shriek and keeled over
backward. The few Crane people who had been brave
enough to remain ran away. The Antelopes borrowed
a blanket and covered the Salamander, and everybody
went to bed. Sunset Tracks said, "That's what I call
real doctoring, real doctoring, not that other kind of
mumbo-jumbo."

During the night, Oriole, who was lying next to the
Flower Girl, saw her sit up, then rise and wander
among the people sleeping on the ground. Oriole was
about to call the girl's mother, then she thought, "Maybe I'd better just watch." She saw the Flower Girl bend
down, then she came back to her bed like a shadow.
Oriole heard her sigh once, and almost right away she
fell asleep.

The next morning, while they were cooking breakfast, Antelope suddenly exclaimed, "Why! here is the packet of quills that the old Porcupine gave me, right in my pack. And I thought I had lost it. I can't understand."

When breakfast was ready Antelope said to Oriole, "How is your little friend this morning?"

"Oh, she is out there, playing with all the children."

"What?"

Sunset Tracks laughed. "I told you this woman looked to me like a real doctor."

When breakfast was over, Coyote Old Man opened his little buckskin sack and took out one of those large cylindrical beads of reddish magnesite that are so rare, and he gave it to the Salamander Woman.

"Thank you, thank you, Grandfather!" Then Salamander got up and walked over to the river. She waded in and disappeared under the water.

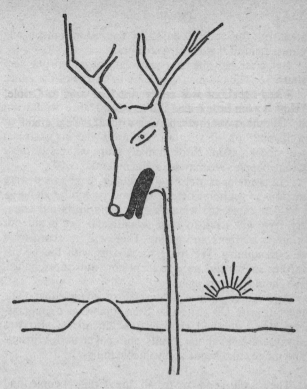

It was time to hold the White Deerskin Performance, but the old men of the village were quarreling. In this dance a line of men stand in a row holding the long poles on which the deerskins with stuffed heads are held, and at each end of the line a man stands a little in front of the others, holding in his hands the large spearheads of obsidian flint that are so rare and valuable. These men who display the great flints are not necessarily the owners; they are usually old men, and it is a great honor to have *your* flints displayed. Well . . . the old men in charge of the dance were quarreling as to whose flints should be displayed. The quarreling

133

went on for several days, to the astonishment and amusement of the desert Antelopes.

But after a while the quarreling began to get very tiresome. The old men who were in charge of the dance sulked in their houses and refused to come out, so it began to look as if the White Deer Dance would not be held that year at all. Grizzly said, "We might as well move on. If we turn northwest and go upstream we will be passing through many more villages of these Crane people. We may see some other dances."

The Antelopes were quite willing to go; they were anxious to get home before autumn was too far along.

"You know, the winter sets in early up in our country. We will have to skip around and get in all our supplies of roots and grains. There are no acorn trees in our country. We trade for acorns with the people farther south, and we give them pine nuts in exchange. We should be starting home."

And Antelope was not averse to going either. The meeting with her sister had been somewhat disappointing. Her sister had changed too much; she also was always talking about insults and payment for insults and money and beads and valuable things.

They said good-by to all the Crane people and started to follow the river upstream to the northwest. A few young Crane people joined their party.

"This quarreling will never stop. We are tired of the old people. We have relatives at Katimin; we will get there in time to see some of the dances."

And now they were going along the trail by the side of the stream. It became a deep canyon with steep walls covered with forests. The Antelopes didn't like it at all.

"What a terrible place. You can hardly breathe. That's all you can see of the sky, that patch of green up there. The people who live here, how do they keep the moss from growing in their hair?"

But there were many people living along this river. Wherever there was a flat place there would be a village of plank houses. They often passed people in boats and people fishing for salmon from platforms built over the stream. There were other places where the river rushed down over rapids, and yet they saw boats shooting down these rapids. The desert Antelopes looked at all this with amazement.

Then they stopped and made camp and ate salmon for supper. After supper one of the young Crane men who had joined the party said, "Tomorrow we will pass Amweykyaara. That's the place where the spirit man stole the salmon and gave it to the world. Then we'll come to Katimin, and that, the old ones say, is the center of the world."

The next morning the Crane man went around to see some of his people, and when he returned he said to the Bear party, "Yes, it is just as I thought. They are going to hold the Deerskin Dance at Katimin. The *isivsaanen pikiavish* has already been in the *wennaram* for several days and everything is ready to make the world."

"Wait a minute, wait a minute," said the Antelope Man who spoke Chinook. "What do these words mean?"

"Well, *isivsaanen* is the world, the acorn trees, the rocks, the deer, the salmon, everything—that's what we call *isivsaanen*. And *pikia,* that means making it. *Pikavan* is one who makes it; he is an old person who is in charge of making the world again every year, just the way it was made in the beginning."

"Didn't Coyote make the world?"

"I don't know anything about that; I never heard anything about Coyote making the world. The world was made by spiritmen and it has to be made again every year, otherwise it will go to pieces, everything will go wrong, the deer will die, and the salmon too, and the acorn trees won't bear any more acorns, and we will all die. That's why that old person who is in charge has been fasting for several days and reciting proper formulas in the *wennarum,* the sacred house, the ceremonial house. And tomorrow he is going to make new fire at Katimin. Every year he makes new fire. It's very important. Everybody will be there. You won't want to miss it."

So the whole party started and soon arrived at Katimin, a village in the bottom of a canyon at the foot of the sacred mountain. They went up the mountain and there they found the person who was making the world, followed by a group of people. That year she was an old woman. She had been preparing for ten days, staying alone in the ceremonial house—and every day she went out and wandered over the mountainside, visiting certain places in the brush, mumbling formulas, thinking; and every day a larger and larger crowd of people, mostly young men and girls, followed her around. She was making the world, and this evening she was going to make new fire.

Now she went up the mountain to a special place, and now a crowd of people was following her. And now she was making new fire by drilling wood. Everybody was watching. The punkwood began to smoke. The Crane Man who had been acting as guide to the Bear party, now said, "When she cries that the flame is ready to catch, you must cover your eyes. Don't look until she says to. It is very dangerous to look."

Now the old woman gave the warning cry, and they all covered their eyes. And now she called again, and they all looked at the flame. Now everybody went down the mountain to the village for the Deerskin Dance, but the old woman who had made new fire stayed on the mountain all night, mumbling formulas, and some stayed with her to help her keep awake. It is not easy to make the world anew.

The next morning the Bear party started traveling upstream again, and by evening they reached Asisfutunik which was the last village of the Crane people. The man who had been their guide had followed them because he had some relatives in the village. That eve-

ning the Bear party asked him if he knew the story of
the two women whose lovers had died and who went
to visit them in the Land of the Dead.

"Of course, I know that story. This is the way it
goes:"

At Katimin they lived long ago, two very good flint-carriers. And at Mahiniva each one had a sweetheart. Then both men got sick, and both of them died. The girls grieved very much.

Near their home a very old woman had died not long before. They used to carry her around on a stretcher. All at once, she said, "Carry me outside." When they had put her down outside, she said, "Look over there across. They are dancing the Deer Dance, the dancers are dancing along the ridge." Then a fog rose where she had been lying and it floated across the river and up the side of the mountain. That old woman had been world-maker ten times.

Every morning early the two girls go out to gather wood. They got to Top-of-the-Bank. That is the place where they stand, the trimmed trees of their lovers, the memorial trees trimmed of all branches except two, pointing to east and west. The girls go there and cry when they look at the trimmed trees.

Summer came at last.

One morning early the girls were there, crying, at the place where they always go. While they were looking at their trimmed trees, all at once someone spoke to them. It was the Bird, the mysterious Bird who lives with his mate near the top of Sugar Loaf Hill. Each year he takes their brood to the Land of the Dead and leaves them there.

"Hey! Are you feeling sad about your lovers?" he asked.

"Yes, yes!"

Then he said, "I had better take you there. I am the only one who goes there where they are now."

And they said, "All right!"

"You can only look at them. They won't come back. But I feel sorry for you whenever I see you crying here." And then he said, "In ten days you must be ready, then you must come early in the morning to Rock Hill Ridge. That is the time I take my children to the Land of the Dead, and I will take you too."

And then at last they counted that ten days had passed. It was the time he had told them to be ready. While it was still dark the Bird's children began calling. When the girls heard them, they too set out at once. Then they sat down at Rock Hill Ridge. They had not been waiting long when they heard the Bird's children calling, and saw them flying past overhead.

Then the Bird called down to them, "You keep traveling along below us."

So they climbed the ridge. And finally at the top they could look far into the distance and see that it was one long ridge, the same as that on which they were walking. And above them the Bird's children were traveling along.

At last they had come a long way. Then, it seemed as though they were going down. The Bird's children said, "We're nearly there." They looked and saw only side hills of brush all around, elderbrush—it was the only kind there was. And when they reached the foot they found a river flowing. And there was also a house. The roof of the house looked grey from all the birds that perched on it.

But no one looked at the girls. Close to the eaves of the house they stood, and the birds who had come with them perched on the roof.

He said to them, the Bird, "Don't go around. Don't go looking around."

But they looked around. There were all kinds of gambling games going on around them. Then at dusk the people made a big fire outside. All around it was swept clear.

Then the one who had brought them, that one said, "This is the only way you can see your lovers. They are going to dance the Deer Dance. Go and stand there, one at each end of the line. There they will be carrying the flints, your lovers." And at both ends of the line they went and stood.

Now they are dancing the Deer Dance. At each end of the line they sit, those two who had been their lovers. Now they stand up, they hold their flints.

Toward them the women stretched their hands. They thought, "I should like to touch you!" They touched nothing. They could only see them.

The dance is nearly over. They stand at the ends, the flint-carriers. And one of them walked over. She thought, "I should like to speak to him!" And then she spoke to him, she said, "Why don't you speak to us? We have come so far! We wanted to see you, we wanted you again!"

He said, "I can't speak to you now. Tomorrow I will speak to you."

So when the dance was over, they went back to where they had first been standing and right there they sat down. At last it grew light. They were still there. They were hungry. No one had come to speak to them as they sat there. Finally the sun came up. They looked around and found themselves in front of a house, and saw that there was an old woman sitting there. Suddenly, the old woman spoke.

"Are you the ones I've heard them speak of, the living ones with bones?"

"Yes, we are," they said.

Then she said, "Where do you come from?"

"From Katimin."

And she said, "I also came from there. I am the one who was world-maker ten times. Then at Rock Hill Ridge I floated up as a fog."

Then they said, "We too came the same way," and they added, "the Bird brought us."

Then she said to them, "Why did you come here?"

They said, "They were our lovers, the two flint-carriers. That's why we came here. We wanted to talk to them."

Then the old woman said, "I don't think you can do it. It's a great pity for you that you have come so far for nothing. And for only two nights you can stay here. All of them, they don't like you. You have bones."

Then she questioned them about everything. "Ka-timin, the country, does it look the same?" Then she said, "I'll make a lunch for you when you leave."

They said, "All right."

Then they stayed the day with the old woman. Right there all around they were playing all kinds of gambling games, but the girls never went near. Then, when it was dark, again they made a big fire. They swept the ground well all around.

Then again, the Bird told them, "Go and stand at the ends of the line when the dance is going on. There they, your lovers, will be carrying the flints."

At last, when they were almost ready to stop, as the girls were standing at the ends of the line again, one of the lovers spoke.

He said, "Where are you staying?"

And she said, "Under the eaves of the old woman's house, that's where we're staying."

Then he said, "We will come there when we have finished."

So when they had finished, the women went back to the house, and soon the men arrived.

Then they said, "It is a great pity that you have come so far for nothing. You can't even touch us. You have bones! There is nothing more that we can say to you."

Then the women told them how they had come

there, how they used to go and cry while they looked at the trimmed trees. And then they said, the lovers, "You should not do that any more. We can never go back there, we have come to have no bones. But, nevertheless, we feel very sad for you. And you must not stay here long. You have bones. And don't eat any food, even if they give it to you." Then the lovers said good-by to them. "And don't grieve for us. We are flint-carriers here, and that is all."

Then the girls said, "We will go back. And we won't eat any food, even if they give it to us."

In the early morning the Bird said, "You must get ready. We are going to leave."

Then they told the old woman, "We are going to leave."

The old woman tied up the lunch. She wrapped it well with brush. Then she said, "Don't lose it. When you get back, whenever you see someone dying, rub this on his lips. Only when this is gone need anyone ever die again. Right away, people will get well when you rub this on their lips."

Then they said good-by to the old woman and they started out. The Bird left all his children there. They traveled back the same way they had come. Above them flew the Bird. At last, when they had gone very far, again it seemed as though they were going downhill. Suddenly, they looked over and saw the hill they called Farthest-out-One and they thought, "We are nearly there!" At Rock Ridge Hill they ran down and they came to Katimin.

The people had been looking for them everywhere. They were crying, they thought the girls had been killed. They were all amazed when they saw these two coming home.

The Bird went back to the top of the Sugar Loaf. That is his home.

As for what the women brought back with them; before long one died near their home, and they rubbed on his lips what had been given them. He came to life.

And indeed, from that time on that's the way it happened. Downstream, far away, everywhere, when anyone died they rubbed it on and he came to life. And also upstream, here and there, they rubbed that on and the people came to life. At last the land on every little creek was occupied and the people were crowded. It was many years before what the old woman had given them was all gone and finally a person died.

The Bird is there yet, and still he takes his children to the land where the spirits go. Only two of them, they live there, one male and one female. Sometimes people kill one of them. Then in only two days another will come to take its place. The feathers are medicine for any kind of sickness that may be around. People carry the feathers of the Bird, so that they won't get sick. That's why from time to time they kill one. . . .

They started again in the morning. Now the river was much smaller; it was no longer running between two walls of steep slopes covered with forest; it began to form a valley. The desert Antelopes began to feel much better.

"Now we can breathe again!" they said.

And now they could see Mount Shasta away over to the east. It looked beautiful, rising all alone, so high, and the very top covered with snow.

"Now we all must make sure that we have good tule slippers," Grizzly said. "For several days we are going to travel through very bad lands; rough going! Even good slippers won't last long on the rocks of this country. We will go around Mount Shasta, to the north of it. There is nobody living in these places. There are only a few springs long distances apart. All that land belongs to no one until we get to the land of the Wolves. We must stick together. No straggling and no going around on side trips, for we might meet a raiding party of Wildcats."

Now they seemed to be on top of the world. The country was flat, and there were open forests of big tall pines. It was a silent and lonely country, and no water anywhere. But the air was crisp and thin.

Now they arrived at really bad lands, lava beds left from ancient volcanoes, black shiny rock everywhere, no trees, no brush, nothing but black shiny rock.

And now they began to get into real sagebrush country, the pungent smell of sage was everywhere. At the

end of a long day's travel they arrived at the shore of a large lake. It was a very large lake, and the shores were covered with tall tule reeds. It was a weird place, no forests to fringe the lake, and the water was brackish, but it was the best they could do.

This was a land of vast horizons—the air was so clear that hills very far away looked quite near. That's why they began to see a range of hills away far in the east. The Antelopes cried, "That's our home! That's where we live, beyond those mountains."

The Antelopes said good-by to the Bear party at the village of Qosale'ta; they were going to their home over the range of mountains. The Bear party proceeded down the river which the Wolves called Adzumma. It could hardly be called a river, its flow was so sluggish. It meandered through the plain which was covered with sagebrush.

They traveled all day, and in the evening they arrived at another village of Wolves, a place called Dalmooma, where there was a hot spring and also a big winter house. And when Fox Boy heard that name, he remembered and he said to Coyote Old Man, "Grandfather, isn't that the name of the place in the doctor's song that says,

> *At Dalmooma by the spring,*
> *I dig for wild turnips.*
> *At Dalmooma in the evening*
> *I dig nothing but rotten ones.*

"Yes," said Coyote, "it goes like this:

> *dal moo ma, hi li ma dai mi . . .*

"That's a song of a Shaman," Coyote said, "a good song, a fine song, full of power."

"Grandfather," Fox Boy said, "will you teach me the songs of the Shaman, good medicine songs full of power? I want to have power!"

"How can I? I'm just an Old Man Coyote. I don't know any."

"Oh, YES you do, Grandfather! You could teach me if you wanted to. You know everything!!"

"All right," grumbled the old Coyote, "but you're just a LITTLE BOY. You won't understand."

Fox sat on a stump and listened with all his might.

These are the songs of the Shaman that Grandfather Coyote sang.

> *Wildcat who stalks the trail alone,*
> *I never yet told of you*
> *And of your bitterness in the brush.*
> *The sun is setting, Wildcat, in the western sea.*

You Snake who never answered me,
Where were you going?
O Snake who never answered me,
When I killed you in the evening.

Across the canyon, you, Coyote,
Across the canyon, you, Coyote,
What are you doing?
When I call you, come.

Fly of autumn crawling on my arm,
Fly of autumn looking for shelter,
Don't you know
That I am going to smash you?

Serpent on the rock, stretched in the sun,
Crawl into your hole
And tell the rain to come:
My heart is drying in my belly.

Raven perching on the dead tree,
Fly to the mother of the sun,

Old-Spider-in-the-sky,
And tell her that my heart
Is slowly freezing under my ribs.

I am Pis'wis'na. I am the Hawk.
I am the Hawk, I cry.
I cannot get rid of the bitterness.
Always I remember.

I am Locust, I never die!
I am a hundred, flashing in the sun.
I am a rattle for the dance.
I am a war song.

A big fly came smelling of me
As I lay rotting in the sun.
Go away, big fly, go away!
Don't bother me, big fly.
I am dreaming.

Busy bee flying back to crowded hive,
You are no totem for shaman seeking power!
I am looking for a locust in the grass,
A locust whirring in the sunlight.

Fox lurking in the night,
I see your eyes.
Go tell the waxing moon
That my mind is dark.

I am Pis'wis'na, the Hawk.
I am myself.
I thought I was myself
But I am only a head.
I am a head crying in the desert.

Worm, you are no totem for shaman!
I am looking for Cocoon Man
Hiding in his house
Counting his power.

A dragonfly came to me
With news from my home.
I lie in the afternoon,
Looking toward the hills.

Turtle woman, turtle woman,
Crawling along
And lifting your head.

Your eyes are blind.
At what do you look?

Green eyes inscrutable,
You were my mother, a snake.
Why did you bite me
Searching in the ferns?

Coyote, my power, come!
Through the wind I call you,
Through the rain, in the storm,
I, a young man, am calling you.
Answer what's in my heart.

I have no bow.
I have nt arrows.
I carry my head in my quiver.

I have no moccasins and nothing around my loins.
I stand headless on the mountain
Crying for power.

You left me! I am crying.
The sand is hot under my foot,
The sun is blinding my eyes.
Where are you, my power?

Grandfather,
  What is that lying half buried in the sand,
  And the wind whistling through
  A strange tune?
Those are Coyote's bones, grandchild,
  Calling, laughing, calling, crying.

Poor Coyote! Let's stick a flower
  Between his ribs.
Good-by, Coyote bones.

  Crying along the trail,
  Packing her cradle board.
  "Hey, Woman, you dropped your burden!"
  "No, I buried him in a tree."

  Sitting by the door
  Making moccasins,
  Thinking about nothing,

The sun is half-way down
At the end of the plain.

I am talking to the lake.
I am talking to all in the lake.
I am not a human being.

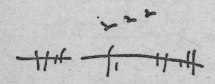

My husband is a werewolf
And my lover did not come tonight.
I am a head rolling down the hill.
I am a head calling for my power.
I run down the mountain,
I come from a lake.
My power is a howling wind.

I lost my belt on the trail,
O snake in the sun.
I'll take you for my gee string,
Young snake in the sun.

I climb the mountain.
I am looking for a crater lake.
Don't anybody follow me, I am in trouble.
I must sing my bitterness to the lake,
Alone.

By the dark pool at sunset
The Puma waits.
The shadows rise, clutching at the night
But I dare not go back.

It was at that place called Dalmooma that the Bear party witnessed a near war between the Wolves and some Wildcats. These Wildcats, about a score of them, had come to demand the return of a young woman of theirs who, they claimed, had been abducted by the Wolves during a raid. These Wildcats were warriors but there were some young women among them, and they were in an ugly mood. It looked as if there might be a fight.

Grizzly, who knew the customs of the north country, advised the Bear party to move their camp a little distance from the village so that it would be apparent to all that they were peaceful strangers and took no sides in the dispute. Antelope, who was nervous, thought maybe it would be better to travel on down the river, but Grizzly and Bear would not hear of it.

"It would look as if we were cowards and were running away," they said.

The children, Fox and Oriole, were all for staying and watching the fight. Coyote Old Man didn't say anything, he always took things calmly, he had seen a lot.

"Anyway, they won't bother us, if we don't take sides," Grizzly added. "Everybody knows by now that we are peaceful travelers. And besides, sister-in-law, we

154

can defend ourselves. We have spears and bows, and I believe these children could fight almost as well as grown-ups; they are growing so fast with all this traveling. I have seen fighting like this before when I was living with these people. It's almost like a wrestling match only it's a little worse. Two or three people will be wounded with arrows but there will be no close fighting with spears. Then everybody will be satisfied and these Wildcats will go home. Of course, of course, somebody might get killed and then there will be a war, but next spring, not now. It's too close to winter. If we left in a hurry now it would look very bad, and I, for one, would never want to come back into this country. I would be ashamed. But you children stick around our camp tomorrow. Don't go visiting with the village people."

They saw the fight the next day. The Wildcat men were armed with bows-and-arrows and they wore a kind of armor made of thick elk hide, rawhide, like a tube, with two holes for the arms. It reached from below the waist to the top of the head, with the part in front of the face cut out. They deployed into a line and started a war song, *YaYAHENNAH* . . .

There were several young women. Each stood behind her man and held onto his belt.

Then the Wolves of the village came out, also in armor. They deployed into another line facing the Wildcats and they also had young women, with them. The two lines stood facing each other at about the extreme range of ordinary bows. They started insulting each other, the Wolves sang their war song, then the arrows began to fly. Most of them fell short but every little while one shot from a powerful bow would break against the elk armor of a warrior. On both sides they did some wonderful dodging.

The warriors held their quivers on the back with the feathered ends sticking out behind the ear, and they reached for them over the left shoulder. Those who had young women behind were lucky because the girls handed them the arrows and when the quiver was empty the girls scooted around picking up arrows from the ground—a difficult thing for a warrior to do in his tube of elk armor.

Sometimes a young fellow who wanted to show off would discard his armor and stand in front of the line to display his skill at dodging. One young Wolf was especially skilled. He would move his body just a little from side to side or lift a knee and let the arrow go under it. The enemies showed a sporting spirit and only one man at a time took him for a target. This was a shooting match and not a real war—in a real war they would shoot from ambush without any play-acting.

The Wolves and the Wildcats kept up the battle for a couple of hours, with several casualties on each side —arrows through the thigh or the arm and a few teeth knocked out. Then each side retired. Later that afternoon one old fellow of the Wildcats came alone to the camp of the Bear party and the Chief of the Wolf village came also. It was evident that both were ready for peace but, of course, they had to have a long argument. The Wolf Chief made the point that the young woman who had been abducted had a man who suited her and she was perfectly willing to stay with the Wolf tribe. He offered to fetch her and if she wanted to go back to her people of her own free will, the Wolves would be satisfied.

When the girl appeared it turned out that she did not want to go back to her people. Her man was a good hunter and they liked each other. The girl was a relative of one of the Wildcat warriors, so the fellow was sent for. He came with several others and when they arrived they all handed their bows-and-arrows to Grizzly. Then several young Wolves came over and they handed their bows-and-arrows to Bear. They sat near Bear, while the Wolves sat near Grizzly, and then they started arguing and wrangling.

It was agreed finally that they would exchange presents because it was the custom in both tribes for the man or his relatives to buy the woman, and for the woman or her relatives to buy the man. The Wolf Man had his eye on the stone pipe that the old Wildcat Man was smoking; it was made of some kind of bluish stone which the Wolves didn't have in their country. The old fellow didn't want to part with it, he said pipes like that were rare and hard to make, but the woman's relative bullied him into giving it. The Wolf didn't have anything with him to give. Here Antelope came to the rescue; she fished in her pack and brought out the little basket with the quail design which she had just finished. Everyone admired it very much, they had never seen any weaving like that in the north country.

When they were departing, the Wildcats said to the Bear party: "You must surely come again next year and visit us and teach our people to weave baskets like that one."

The next morning a young Wolf, the one who had shown so much daring and skill in dodging arrows during the shooting match, came over to the camp of the Bear party. He was a lively, simple young fellow, full of curiosity. He kept asking all sorts of questions about the people who lived in the south country and their customs, saying wistfully, "How I wish I could travel and see other places!" His name was Suwasaqtseemi tsimmu, which meant, "I dreamed about a wolf," but they called him simply Tsimmu for short.

The children liked Tsimmu. He and Fox Boy got into long discussions about who had been the first people on the earth and how the world was made, anyhow. That was a question which was always bothering Fox Boy no end. Oriole Girl was impressed by Tsimmu's bravery.

"Weren't you afraid to stand there in front of the line and dodge the arrows without even any armor?"

He laughed.

"No, if I were afraid, that would be the end of me. You have to keep cool, and if you are afraid, you can't

be cool. You see, it's the arrows that come at your eyes
that you have to watch for. The others that come at
your legs or arms don't matter so much, but when one
flies straight at you and all you can see of it is just a
black dot like a bee, then look out. That one is making
for you between the eyes. Then is the time to squat and
let it go over your head."

When the Bear party was ready to travel again,
Tsimmu looked sad. He kept saying, "Oh, how I wish I
could go with you and see new countries!"

"Well, here is your chance," Bear said. "Come with
us. You know the country until this river comes
down out of the mountains and turns south into the
great valley, so you can help us find our trail. From
there on, we know the way. You can spend the winter
with us. The winters are easy in our country."

"That would be fine," said the young Wolf. "I've
always wanted to travel, but I was afraid to go alone
among strangers, not knowing their ways. They might
kill me."

"No, we are peaceful people. We don't make war on
strangers."

"Oh, it's not FIGHTING people I am afraid of, but
what about your doctors?"

"What do you mean?" Bear said. "You don't need
to be afraid of our doctors."

"No? Well, it's different with us. Doctors are not
supposed to use their power to make people sick, but
some of them do. Sometimes it's because they are mean
and have a grudge against you; sometimes it's because
someone is sick and that person's relatives take it into
their heads that you are the cause of it; then they'll
prevail upon a doctor who is also a relative to use his
power against you and make you sick by his thinking.
That's why I don't like to go among strangers; I may
do something wrong without meaning to, just because I
am ignorant of their customs. Then they'll get a doctor

to use his power against me, and I wouldn't even suspect it."

Bear laughed at this speech.

"No, we haven't anything like that in our country. Our doctors are not like that. Isn't that so, Grandfather Coyote?"

"I don't know," Coyote said. "I'm not a doctor!"

"Oh, there you go again, always saying that! Do you think you are fooling anybody? We all know you are one of the best doctors in all the world!"

Then Coyote said, "Well, I'll tell you, it *used* to be that way in the south country just as it is here now in the north country. That was long ago, long, long, very long ago. Then things changed, people changed, and the doctors too, just like everything else."

Antelope said, "There is still some of that in our country too. What else is the kind of doctor we call the *madu?*"

This made Coyote Old Man laugh, but Bear looked uneasy. "Oh, you talk too much because you know too much because you are a member of the secret society. I don't like the secret society!"

Grizzly was taking it all in but he didn't say anything or ask any questions, but the young man, Tsimmu, said, "I think I'll take a chance. You make me want more than ever to visit your country."

Antelope smiled at him.

"You seem to be a good dodger. You needn't be afraid."

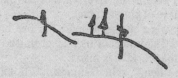

The Bear party left the village of Dalmooma and followed the river going westward. And now they were glad that Tsimmu, the Wolf, had come with them, because the river was becoming quite a stream. In some places it went through deep gorges. The country was changing; it was no longer a plateau of sagebrush and deserts, it was now covered with forests. It was a rough land. And the young Wolf showed them how to take a short cut and rejoin the river farther to the west and save several days of rough travel.

When they were sitting around the fire one evening Fox reminded Tsimmu that he had promised to tell the story of how the world was made.

"All right, then," said Tsimmu, "I'll tell you the creation story—at least, one of them, because, I tell you, I have heard many different ways of telling it. But,

I warn you, it's a long story. I will tell some of it tonight until I get sleepy and the rest tomorrow:"

... There was no world, there was no land. Everywhere was fog, water-foam and clouds. There was no sunlight to make shadows. Cocoon Man was the only person living. He was drifting around for an infinity of time, thinking and dreaming.

Then one day, looking in the direction of the sunrise, he noticed some white foam dirfting down the wind. He watched it all summer. It was far off and did not come near him. Sometimes it floated near, then the wind drove it off again.

Now he tried by the power of his thought to make it come near him; he tried by thinking; he thought again, "Come hither." But it did not come. Now the

Cocoon Man started to sing and stomp and dance.
Then he rested. Then he sang again. Then he rested
again. He did like that for a long time, for an infinity
of time—for ten times ten times ten times ten years.

Then one day the cloud of water-foam drifted near
enough so Cocoon Man jumped on it. Now he drifted
around with the cloud for another infinity of time. Then
one day, he noticed that he had hands and feet because
the water-foam was drying and caking over them. He
never had noticed them before. He saw that all his
body was covered with a crust of the dried-up foam.
So he scratched himself, and the crust dropped off his
body. Then he thought, "I'll shut my eyes and see what
happens." He shut his eyes, and when he opened them
again he saw that the crust had become earth.

That crust that he had scratched off his body had
fallen around him, and he was standing on it, like a
small piece of land floating in a world of foam and
fog. It tilted one way and then another. Then it shook a
little and then it settled. It was like a three-cornered
island. One corner was in the direction of the sunrise;
another in the direction of the sunset, and the third
corner was in the direction of the downstream wind,
the warm wind from the south.

The Cocoon Man then sang and stomped some
more, then he shut his eyes again, and when he looked,
the three-cornered island had become bigger. He was
standing in the center and he could hardly see the
corners.

Now he started to travel around and he found a boy.
That was Annikadel. That was his name; I don't know
what it means, but it sounds something like "living
with," or "living in company." Cocoon Man asked the
boy who he was, but the boy didn't answer. He was a
very small boy, very, very small, just tiny. Cocoon
Man picked him up and put him in his bosom.

Then he traveled on. Then he found another boy. It
was the same boy, but he had shot ahead of Cocoon

Man, and Cocoon Man didn't know it. Cocoon Man asked him who he was, but the boy didn't answer. So Cocoon Man picked the boy up and put him in his bosom and went on.

"Now there are three of us," Cocoon Man thought, and went on. He had reached the western corner, and now he traveled in the direction of the warm wind from the south. After a while he found another boy. It was the same boy again, but Cocoon Man didn't know it. Cocoon Man asked him, "Can you talk?"

"Yes," said the boy, who was Annikadel.

"Then say something!"

The boy said, "When you were in the middle of the world you found me and put me in your bosom. Then you went to the end of the world and you found me again, and you put me in your bosom and you went on. Then you came here to another end of the world and you have found me again. I fooled you. I belong to the air. I am the one who makes sounds in the head. You thought you had made the world but it is I who put the idea into your head."

Cocoon Man was so surprised he almost fainted. . . .

The next day in the evening after supper, the young man, Tsimmu, the Wolf, continued the story of Cocoon Man and how he made the world:

. . . Annikadel said to the Cocoon Man, "There are three persons you have to find. Now, you go around the world, and when you find them send them to the center."

So Cocoon Man started and when he got to one corner of the world he found Alium—she was a woman, a Frog person. Cocoon Man told her to go to the middle of the world. Then Cocoon Man continued on his way and at the next corner he met Kuan, he was a Silver Fox person.

"Go to the middle of the world and wait for me," he said to him. And he travelled on. At the last corner he found Dzeemul—he was Coyote. "Where are you going?" he asked Coyote.

"I dunno," said Coyote. "I am traveling, I am going around. I was worried about something. I thought I might meet somebody."

"All right," said Cocoon Man. "Go to the middle of the world and wait for me."

Then that Cocoon Man went away, and *nobody ever saw him again.* But Silver Fox, Frog Woman and Coyote met each other in the center of the island. The world was still shaking and rocking a little, so the Silver Fox, who was all black with silver hair, said to Coyote, "You would better go and fix the world firmly. It's rocking too much. Make three posts and set them firmly in the ground at each corner of the world."

So Coyote went. He couldn't find anything to make posts out of except the rainbow, so he split the rainbow in three and drove the posts at each corner. But the posts kept shifting around, so Coyote went back and complained to Silver Fox. Silver Fox then made some tule reeds come by his thinking, and he gave those to Coyote. Coyote then returned to the corners of the world and tried to drive the sticks of tule into the ground, but they kept bending and breaking.

So Coyote went back to the middle of the world and complained again to Silver Fox. But Silver Fox only smiled and squinted his eyes. He said, "You are stupid. You don't know how to do anything. Never mind. The world seems to be settling down, anyhow, and I don't think it will move any more."

Coyote said, "What are we going to do now?"

"Go around again, and see if you can find more people."

"No, I can't go. I have to have some water. I'm hungry."

"No, you don't need any water."

"I tell you, I'm hungry. I haven't anything in my belly. I'm getting weak."

"No, you don't need anything in your belly. You'll travel better." Then he gave Coyote a cane of tule reed and said, "Here, suck this if you are hungry and thirsty." So Coyote put it in his mouth and chewed on it and felt better. Then he started to travel.

He traveled in the direction of the sunset for some time. Then he heard voices ahead of him, behind a hill. He went around the hill, but there was no one there. Now he heard the same voices on the other side of the same hill, so he ran around, but he found no one. Then he heard the same voices again on the other side of the hill, and again he ran around the hill in the other direction as fast as he could, but he found no one. They were Lan, Wild Goose people. Silver Fox had made them come by his thinking, just to fool Coyote.

Coyote never found them. Silver Fox knew it, but when Coyote went back, Silver Fox said, "Did you meet anybody?"

"Yes, I found some people and they asked me who I was. I told them I was a doctor, a mean one, and I was making the world, fixing it right, the way it used to be."

"When was that?" asked Silver Fox.

"I dunno," said Coyote.

Silver Fox didn't say anything, he only squinted and smiled.

Tsimmu yawned. "I'm sleepy now. I'll tell you the rest some other time."

They were now in the foothills, which were rougher than the mountains they had passed. They were still following the same river which went through heavily forested country. Finally they passed the last village of the Wolves and emerged from the foothills onto the plain, or rather a series of shelves covered with high brush. The earth was reddish everywhere and it was oppressively hot, although this was already the middle of autumn. The people no longer wore any buckskin clothes, and the men wore their hair in a net instead of twisted on top of the head and pinned with a wooden hairpin.

Tsimmu asked, "To whom does this land belong?" He had never been beyond the last village of the Wolves.

Grizzly said, "This land here doesn't belong to any one people especially, but it's not an empty desert like the land between you Wolves and the Wildcats. You can see this is good land with good hunting, good fishing, acorns, and lots of wild roots. Everybody claims it and it belongs to nobody. But down here people are peaceful; they don't fight; and if it looks like the beginning of a war, everybody goes back to the foothills or the mountains, to his own home, and waits until the trouble is over."

Tsimmu said, "It must be nice to live like that! A man could grow fat all over his bones. I am tired of always watching for raiding Wildcats!"

"Don't you ever raid THEM?" Oriole asked.

"What for? What could we do with the captives? THEY sell the captives up north to other people who use them as slaves, but WE don't keep slaves."

"Then what do you do with captives?"

"We marry them. Those we don't marry we kill, that is, if they don't kill us first. IT's NOT our fault."

After supper Tsimmu continued the story of the creation of the world.

After a while, Coyote said, "What are we going to do now?"

"Go and travel again," Silver Fox said.

"No, I am tired. You make me work too hard. Besides, I don't want to go alone. I'm tired of traveling alone. It always was that two people travel together. That's the way it used to be."

"When was that?" asked Silver Fox.

"I dunno," said Coyote.

Then Frog Woman spoke. She said, "How would it be for me to travel along with you?"

Coyote said, "Naw, I don't need a woman. What I need is something to put in my belly. I tell you, I'm awfully hungry."

So Silver Fox took pity on him and gave him another cane of tule to chew on, and he started. This time he went in the direction of the warm wind. After a while he met a person. It was Frog Woman—Silver Fox had sent her. He had made her take a long leap through the air and land in front of Coyote. But this was a much younger woman; Coyote did not recognize her. He asked her who she was, but she didn't answer. Coyote asked her again, but she didn't answer. And again. Then Coyote got mad. He said, "You'd better answer me; I am a great doctor, a mean one. If you don't answer me, I'll run my doctor's cane through you and kill you," and he threatened her with the stick of tule that he was chewing. Still she didn't answer, so Coyote ran her through with his cane and went on.

"That's the way it used to be done in the old days," he said.

This time he traveled in the direction of the sunrise. Now he met another woman. It was the same Frog, but he didn't recognize her. She spoke to him first, she said, "Where are you going and why are you traveling."

"Because I am a great doctor. I am the one who made the world, only it isn't just right yet, and I am fixing it."

She said, "You are a liar! You are not a doctor at all. You are nothing but Coyote. I met you back there a while ago and you thought you had killed me. You don't know anything. You don't even know I was the same one!"

Coyote was mad. He tried to grab her, but she jumped on a whirlwind and disappeared.

Then Coyote went back to the middle of the world. Silver Fox asked him, "Did you find anyone?"

"Yes, I found several young girls and married them. Now we'll have people in this world. It won't be so lonely."

He had not noticed Frog Woman when he came back; he had never taken any notice of her. Now he looked at her and thought he recognized her but he wasn't sure.

"Have I seen you before?" he asked her.

"Have I seen you before?" she repeated.

Coyote said, "No, you never saw me before."

She repeated, "No, you never saw me before."

Silver Fox didn't say anything; he was squinting and smiling. Coyote began to suspect that they were making fun of him. He said, "I am going out to search for something to eat, since you won't feed me anything. That tule is not nourishing enough for me, what with all the hard work I do for the world!"

Silver Fox took pity on Coyote.

"All right," he said, "go out a little way and you'll find something to eat. Go out in the direction of the cold wind. Take this sack which I wove out of tules while you were gone. You will come to a wall of rimrock—"

Coyote interrupted, "How do you know there are rimrocks there? You've never been there."

"All right, then, don't go. I only wanted to help you. I am not hungry myself."

"I only wanted to make sure that you knew what you are talking about," Coyote said. "That's all. Now tell me what to do when I get there?"

Silver Fox said, "You are a great doctor, you can make *waHats* bread come just by calling."

"What's bread?"

"It's something to eat. Stand under the rimrocks, hold the sack open and call 'Bread, come!' But don't eat any there, bring it here to us because this woman and I are also beginning to get hungry so we will share the bread. NOW remember, don't eat it there, bring it here!"

"You don't need to tell me so many times," said Coyote.

He went, and when he arrived at the foot of the wall of rimrocks he sat down and thought for a while. "I wonder if this is dangerous. I never heard of bread before. People never ate bread before." He thought some more. "Bah! it can't be dangerous. Anyhow, I'm a great doctor, I'm a mean one, I'm not afraid of anything."

Coyote got up and stood under the rimrocks with his sack open. He looked up—he couldn't remember that word for bread, *waHats*. He thought, "What was it he said for me to call? Oh yes, now I remember. Come, bread, come, bread!" he called at the top of his voice, holding the sack open. A lot of rocks came down on top of his head. One big rock nearly split his head open.

Coyote went back to the middle of the world. He was limping and his head hurt badly. Silver Fox and the Frog Woman had gone away. Coyote couldn't find them, so he started to travel around in search of them.

Silver Fox and Frog Woman had gone away, so Coyote couldn't bother them again. They found a place and stayed there. One day they noticed a cloud hovering far away near the horizon. It had a queer shape, and they wondered what it was, why it looked like that. They watched it for a long time; then they got tired of watching it and they went to sleep.

When they woke up, the cloud had covered all the sky. And they heard somebody singing in the cloud. It sounded like a young woman's voice; but they couldn't see anybody up there.

A lu, a lu, a si, a lu . . .

Frog Woman said, "It sounds as if someone said 'I am a woman cloud, I am the mother of water.' It's going to rain! You are the cause of that! You dreamed it on purpose." Silver Fox didn't answer anything. He only smiled.

Soon it started to rain. Silver Fox and Frog Woman found a cave in the rocks and went to sleep inside. When they came out again, the rain had stopped and there was a spring of water gurgling out of the rocks.

"There is the water that Coyote wanted," said Silver Fox.

Near the spring there was a young woman sitting on a rock.

"Are you the one who was singing in the cloud?" they asked.

"Yes, I am the one," she said.

"Have you come down to live with us?" they asked.

"No," she said, "I am a person of the air. I cannot live with you. I must go back to where I belong, but I took pity on you because you were thirsty and the earth is thirsty. Somebody sent me."

Silver Fox asked, "Who sent you?"

She answered, "The same one who makes sounds in our heads, the one who makes words. Now I have to go. My name is Aluta, but when I travel through the air I am *Lawiidza*." Then they saw she was an Eagle Woman, and she flew away.

After Lawiidza, the Eagle Girl, flew off, Silver Fox and Frog Woman lived in that place. They were wondering what had happened to Coyote.

"He will come back some day and bother us again. Just wait," they said to each other. Meantime, green things had started to come out of the ground; and some of them grew higher and had berries on them; and some still higher and became trees, bearing acorns and pine nuts. But there wasn't very much light. It was half dark all the time. After a long while it clouded over again, and they heard the Cloud Song.

Then it rained and after the rain they found the Eagle Girl sitting by the spring. They said to her, "This world is all right, now, and things are growing, but we wish there would be more light. We cannot see very well in this half-light. How is it in the upper air where you live? Is there more light there?"

"Yes, there is more light there, but I don't know where it comes from. However, I will go back there to my home and try to find out. When I have found out, I will return. Maybe there is a way to fix it so that there will be more light." Then she flew off again.

She didn't come back for a long time, but when she returned she said, "I found out where the light comes from, what little we have of it. It comes from another world. Two people live there. Their name is Tsulh. I went there but I couldn't get near, not near enough to talk plainly. They seemed to be quarreling. It must be a man and a woman. THEY have plenty of light, but they don't want to leave their place and come to this world with it. I shouted to them, but they wouldn't listen to me. I think we will have to trick them if we want to make them come here." Then the Eagle Girl flew away.

After she had gone, Silver Fox thought hard for a long time, then he went to sleep. When he woke he said to Frog Woman, "I have dreamed of a way to trick those two people, but you will have to help me. When Eagle Girl comes again, we will ask her to take you away up to where the Whirlwind lives. Then you jump on the Whirlwind and ride it to that other world where the two persons Tsulh live. You hang onto the Whirlwind and make it get behind these two. Then, when they start to quarrel, turn the Whirlwind loose on them, and push them along until you get to this world. It's easy."

But Frog Woman didn't want to do it. She was afraid. She said, "Why don't you do it yourself?"

"Because I have to stay here to take care of this place until you come back."

"I'll take care of it," she said, "while you are gone."

But he said no, that he was afraid Coyote might come back, and he wanted to be there to handle him.

"I can handle him better than you can," Frog Woman said. And they argued and argued like that for a long time, until Eagle Girl came back. When Eagle Girl saw that they were still arguing, she said, "I'd better take you both there. You can settle it when we get there."

So they both flew with Eagle Girl. She took them to a place where the Whirlwind was sure to pass, and when he came through, whirling, they jumped on him and hung on. Silver Fox and Frog Woman got very dizzy. Each one was giving the Whirlwind different directions. Finally the Whirlwind split in two. Eagle Girl fell down in between, but she could fly. Now Silver Fox was riding one Whirlwind, and Frog Woman was riding the other, and both of them were giving different directions, each one with a Tsulh in front of them. But Eagle Girl was flying ahead, and the Whirlwinds were following her. That's the way they came back to this world, driving the Tsulhs ahead of them. Finally, the Whirlwinds got tired and came close to the ground, and then Frog Woman and Silver Fox jumped off. But the two Tsulhs never got back together. They are still mad at each other. One has more light than the other. One is day-sun, *matiktsa tsulh,* the other is night-sun, *maHiktsa tsulh.* . . .

"Which one is the man and which one the woman?" asked Fox Boy.

"Nobody knows," said Tsimmu. "At least, I never heard anybody say, not any of the old people. What does it matter? Maybe they are both men, maybe they are both women. Who knows? You have seen earth worms, haven't you?"

"Yes," said Fox Boy.

"Well, then you tell me which is man and which is woman."

Everybody laughed, and they all went to bed.

Now the Bear party traveled south. The land was flat, covered with high grass; but at this time of autumn it was dry and sere and looked almost white—in places it even shone in the sunlight. They had started at the very first dawn, yet by the time the sun was halfway up in the sky the day had become oppressively warm, so they dragged along, hot and thirsty. On the west side there was a wall of mountains, and on the other side of the valley, another wall, but so far away that the mountains were almost lost in the haze.

At noon they came to a creek. It was almost dry, just a little water trickling along in the center of a bed that was more than a hundred yards wide. They ate in silence; they felt too limp to talk. After the high plateaus and the mountains, it was depressing. The Wolf, Tsimmu, felt the heat most, but he never complained. Bear said, "We'd better start again. We'll go as far as we can today and try to reach another creek before sundown. Then in the morning we'll follow it upstream into the foothills, and we'll soon be in the mountains again."

So they shouldered their packs and traveled on again all afternoon, and they did reach another creek by sundown. They camped there and the next day they started to climb the wall of mountains. They climbed all day, and late in the afternoon they arrived on top.

"Now we are in our land," said Bear. "It's not *our own home* yet—we have to travel several days more before we reach our own home—and these are not exactly our own people, but they are not so very different from us. Anyhow, we are out of that valley where we couldn't breathe. The air is better here. It's not such a big high country as where the Wolves and the Antelopes and Wildcats live, but it's mountains, anyway."

It was, in fact, a plateau, a land of many ridges and small secluded valleys, and many mountain lakes with ducks and geese and pelicans and herons and cranes flying about. They traveled south through that upland for several days.

Bear was in a hurry now. He wanted to get home before the winter set in. When they came to a large village on the shores of a lake, a village with a large underground ceremonial house and many huts of brushwood and pine bark, he stopped to salute the chief. His own village was not very far away, half-hidden in a fold of the hills. It was a very pleasant place with oak trees and pines, laurels and shrubs in clumps, and through it a small creek of clear water ran down to the lake. There were just a few houses there, individual houses, no big hall for ceremonies as at the main village.

Well, they were glad to get home at last after all their wanderings of the summer. But it was not long before Bear started worrying, as usual. Now he was worrying because the house was too small for all of them. It was hardly a house. In fact, it was not much more than a lot of sticks and poles joined together at the top and covered with branches and slabs of bark.

"I don't see how we all are going to live in this hut through the winter," Bear said. "The rains are going to start soon. It's all right now to camp in the open, but it will be very uncomfortable in the rain."

"Well, why don't we build a new house then?" asked Grizzly.

"That's what I have been thinking, but I ought to go and ask permission from the chief, first."

"What chief?"

"The one who lives in the big village."

"Well, go and see him then."

But Bear hesitated.

"What's the matter now?" Grizzly and Tsimmu asked.

"Well, it's this way. The real chief is Turtle Old Man, but he is too old, nobody pays any attention to him, and anyway, he will want everything done the old way. If we do it the regular way, we will have to invite everybody to come and help us."

"Well! that would be fine! Put up the house in no time."

"No," Bear said, "it will never get done that way. We'd have to send invitation sticks around and it would be a couple of months before the people arrive, and by that time the rains will have started."

Antelope said to Bear, "Turtle Old Man is not really chief here; he is only chief by courtesy. Why, you don't know your own people! The real chief by rights is a woman. Her father was the chief in his time, but she is only a young woman yet, so the big fellow at the main village is acting as chief. He is her uncle but on her father's side, so that doesn't count. It should go to Turtle Old Man because he is her uncle on her mother's side."

Tsimmu was laughing silently.

"What's the matter?" they asked him.

"Oh, I am laughing because you sound just exactly like my own people, always arguing as to *who* is really chief. There are always five or six old men who are supposed to be chiefs, but they themselves claim they are not. They say it's too much trouble, and anyhow, what's the use, because the young people won't listen to them and they'll do what they want to in the end. I guess it's about the same everywhere."

Here Grizzly spoke up: "Are we going to build a new house or not? We don't need any chief's permission. I am the chief of the visiting tribe, I represent Coyote Old Man, Tsimmu the Wolf, and this young woman Oriole, and I order a house to be built right away!"

Antelope said, "That's the way to talk, brother-in-law. I wish I had married you instead of this old-fashioned man of mine who never can make up his mind."

"Well, you can marry him yet, you know," Bear growled.

Grizzly chuckled, "So the long and the short of it is I have to kill my brother Bear so as to get this Antelope."

"Stop all this nonsense and get to work," said Antelope. "Here, everybody, let's get to work. I have my digging-stick and you fellows can make your own. And there are plenty of baskets to carry the dirt."

Tsimmu was already sharpening the point of a digging-stick in the fire by burning the end and then rubbing off the burned part. Fox Boy and Oriole went into the woods with Grizzly to look for suitable sticks. Grandfather Coyote went off, saying he was going to report them to Turtle Old Man, but what he really wanted was an excuse to get out of work and to gossip with his old friend. Bear was still sitting down. Antelope called to him, "What are you waiting for? Why don't you go to the rimrocks and call, 'House, come rolling down!' "

"Oh, leave me alone, woman. I am deciding in my mind just where to start the digging, but I can't think if you bully me. We want a spot where there'll be sure to be good drainage. That's the first thing to be sure of."

"What about that flat there?"

So they went to work digging. They excavated a place about twenty feet wide, dumping the dirt around the rim. By midafternoon when Grandfather Coyote and Turtle Old Man arrived to give their opinion, the excavation was already waist-deep. Of course, Turtle Old Man had to grumble and criticize the choice of location, but they only grinned at him and went on with their digging.

Then Bear went into the woods to look for a center-post. A redwood was best, but as the white sap-wood rotted right away and only the inside heart was good, it took an enormous tree to make a center-post, a tree so large that two men could scarcely circle it with their arms. They would have to work all summer to fell such a tree. Old Man Coyote suggested that they use madronyo; it wouldn't last as long, but it was good and strong.

They found one, and after several days of continual burning and chiseling and scraping, they cut through the stump and dragged home the tree. Then they cut a ridgepole and rafters. Bear had decided not to use the smoke-hole as a door, so they dug one through the rampart of earth around the excavation. Now they were ready to lay down the roof of large slabs of pine bark and to cover it with earth. Soon grass would be growing on the roof.

Now the house was finished and they could live in it.

"And it's a good thing, too," said Bear. "The rains are liable to start any time now. What moon are we in, Antelope?"

"I'm sure it is the fourth moon after the fifth," Antelope said.

"How do you people make your moons come out right?" asked Tsimmu. "How do you keep your night moons from getting ahead of your sun moons? We have ten and three moons in our year and every fourth year we drop one of them."

"We do the same thing," Antelope said in a low voice.

"How come you know and my brother Bear doesn't?" Grizzly asked.

"Because he doesn't pay any attention to those things," Bear said. "Antelope is a member of the secret society. She is a *matutsi*. They are interested in things like that."

"We have no secret society with our people," Tsimmu said. "We all know those things, but, of course, the old men know more than the young ones. When we want to see if it is midwinter, somebody goes out and sets up a stick in the snow just in line with the sun at sunset. Then if the next day the sun sets south of it, they know for sure that midwinter is yet to come."

Antelope said, "You don't need a stick. All you need to do is watch at sunset and notice what company of stars the sun sets in."

"Goodness, do you know all the companies of stars? I know only one, the one we call *wallustsi,* a bunch of little stars together. And, of course, I know the north star. Everybody does."

Tsimmu stared at the fire and everybody was silent for a while, then Fox Boy said, "My goodness, but the world is complicated! I am going to join the secret society and learn!"

Grandfather Coyote laughed.

"You'd better wait until you are initiated, young fellow. It's almost time for you to go to the mountain and look for a protector, for a *tinihowi*. You have to go to the mountain at sunset. Run to the top, fast, try to beat the sun to the top. Spend the night there. Spend two or three nights there. Don't take any food with you. Don't come back until you get a *tinihowi*. Some fellows go kind of crazy. If someone comes near them they run away or throw rocks at you—won't let you come near them."

"Did you do that?"

"Sure, I did! Do you suppose I wanted to go back without a *tinihowi* and be just a no-account man?"

"Did you get a *tinihowi?*" asked Oriole.

"Sure, I did! I got a wolf. I had gone to sleep on the shore of a mountain lake in the afternoon. It was an awful place, lonesome place, water looked all black. Then somebody pushed my head and I woke up. It was that wolf pushing my head with his foot. And he said, 'What are you doing here, young fellow? Go home to your people, they are crying for you. I took pity on you. I'll help you. Listen, this is my song.' And he sang his song for me. 'And when you want me, come here and sing my song. I'll hear you and I'll come. Now jump into the lake. You'll die but I'll take you out. Don't be afraid.'

"Well, that lake looked awful. The sun was setting and the water looked like all kinds of fire. But I jumped into it."

"But you didn't die!" cried Fox.

"Why, certainly I died."

"How can you have died since you are here?"

"That wolf took me out, just like he said he would."

"I don't believe it!!!" said Fox.

"YOU don't believe anything ever," said Oriole. "Remember Doctor Loon, and Doctor Salamander, and what happened to you that time when you were looking for a yew tree?"

"How do you know THAT? I NEVER TOLD YOU!"

"Maybe you talked in your sleep, silly. That's what happens to little boys when they sleep under the same rabbit-skin blanket with a girl. Girls are curious and they listen."

"Oh, you are a great one to tell me that I never believe! Just the other day you told me that I ought to believe anything I liked."

"That's not the same as not believing anything you don't like."

"How is that again?"

"Oh, never mind! Grandfather Coyote, will you tell

us the story about your great-great-grandfather and the
little louse girl? You said you would."

"All right," said Coyote Old Man.

. . . Grandfather Coyote was going across the hills
to visit another village. On the way he met a little girl.
She was Louse. Coyote called her: "Little abalone-
shell, where are you going?" She didn't answer. "Are
you going west?" No answer. "Are you going south?"
No answer. "Are you going east, are you going north?"
No answer. Coyote got mad. "Are you going into my

tail?" and he waved his tail in front of her. It wasn't a
very good tail—it was kind of ragged and not much
hair on it. But Louse Girl nodded yes, and she climbed
on it and Coyote kept on his way and forgot all about
her.

But he hadn't gone very far before his tail began to
itch. So he rubbed and rubbed himself against a tree.
But it only made it itch all the more. So he rubbed it
with a piece of bark. Itched all the more. Coyote got
mad. He looked around for a rock. He found one the
size of his fist. Then he laid his tail on a tree stump
and he pounded, and pounded, and pounded his tail
away. "Heh! that's the way to do it! that's the way they

used to do in the old days. *Nin ikgima-haaba 'am ki kuui yehelsa.*" And he went on.

But now his leg began to itch so he looked around for a rock and he laid his leg on a stump and he pounded, and pounded it away! "Heh! *Nin ikgima-haaba 'am ki kuui yehelsa.*" And he went on, hopping on one leg.

And now the other leg started to itch. So he looked around for a rock, and sitting himself on the stump he pounded his leg away. *"Nin ikgima-haaba 'am ki kuui yehelsa,"* and he lost his balance and rolled off the stump and he crawled on his way, pulling himself along with his forelegs. But his arms were itching now. So he pounded off one arm. And he went on toward the north, dragging himself with just one foreleg.

And still it itched! Now Coyote got mad. . . . He grabbed a rock and laid his head on another rock and pounded his own neck and pounded and pounded his head away. Coyote's head started rolling down the hill, rolling, rolling, rolling down the hill.

Some children were playing a little way from the village. When they saw the head rolling downhill toward them they were frightened and ran home. "Some kind of monster is taking a walk over there." The chief of the village said: "We ought to investigate." Two brave young men volunteered to go. When they returned they said: "Some kind of monster it is! It is rolling along on the ground." The chief said: "Catch it in a net or in a basket." So they took a basket and laid it on the trail. The head rolled into it, and the two men brought it to the village. They took it into the ceremonial house and deposited it at the foot of the center-post, on the south side. Then the head hopped out of the basket.

"Bring me your beads, bring me all your money!" said the head. So the people went to their houses and returned with their beads and piled them up at the foot of the center-post; it made quite a big pile. Then the head said: "Leave it here for a while. I'll return in a second!" Then the head rolled out of the ceremonial house, rolled out of the village, rolled back to the place where it had hacked itself loose from the neck and reattached itself to it. Then it went on dragging itself with one foreleg back to the place where it had hacked off the other one. Then back to the place where one hindleg was lying by the side of the trail. Then it hopped back to the other leg. Then he ran back to the tail and reattached it on. NOW it was Coyote once more, a person. And he ran back to the village and went into the ceremonial house to get his beads.

But Bluejay cried: "I suspected all along that it was another trick of Master Coyote!" Coyote didn't say anything. He just squinted and smiled. "Boys," he said: "lend me a basket!" "There is one over there—don't you see it?" "Where? where?" "There, over there, outside." Coyote went out to look for the basket. When he returned, the people had taken back all their beads and gone home to their houses. And Coyote was going around the village as usual, begging for food . . .

Everybody laughed. "That's the end," finished Coyote, "but the real end of a story is to say this: *'sholwat bolwat yolwat buhulwat . . . shoooo . . . cayan hee bek gurkasikasi pi kha'a he'e whiae shobakigagam.'* From the west, from the south, from the north, from the eeeeast, the ducks are flying low over the lake and unfolding the dawn. That's because in the old days they used to tell one story after another all night long until the dawn."

"Goodness!" cried Oriole. "WHEN did they sleep?"

"When they didn't tell stories, Smarty," said Fox.

That autumn there was an initiation of the boys in the large village by the lake. There had not been one for four or five years, and some of the young men who had not been initiated were almost grown up. So the chief and his four assistants sent invitation sticks to all the smaller villages for scores of miles around.

So the Bear family traveled to the village of Big-Mountain-by-the-water, and when they arrived the chief gave them the formal speech of welcome in the traditional staccato high voice, then he dropped his voice to the ordinary manner and said, "Bear, your cousin arrived yesterday with his woman and their daughter. They are camped over there. I guess you'll go and join them. Lots of people are arriving. We'll have a good initiation."

On the way over, Bear said to Grizzly, "That man to whose camp we are going, his mother and our mother were sisters, so I call him brother. That makes his wife our 'teasing relation.' I don't know whether you have that custom up north."

Grizzly said, "You mean when we see her after an absence we must tease her and she must tease us back? Yes, sure, we have the same custom. It's that way everywhere I have been in all the tribes."

That sister-in-law of Bear and Grizzly was a great big fat handsome woman. She was sitting by the camp-fire stirring the acorn mush, dropping hot rocks into the mush and stirring it with a paddle. She turned a volley of jokes and teasing remarks on Bear and Grizzly, who paid back as best they could. That was strictly according to custom, but it was evident she did not need any custom to be a jolly old tease. She hugged Fox Boy, who asked her, "Where is my little cousin, Rhal-pitau?" Rhal-pitau, "the White Bead," was the name of her little daughter.

"Oh, she is somewhere around. Go and find her and tell her to come and help me."

Fox went. When he had gone the White Bead's mother sighed and said to the others, "I don't know what's the matter with that daughter of mine. She is always mooning around by herself, singing sad songs instead of playing with the other children. Maybe she is sick, maybe somebody poisoned her, maybe she lost her shadow, maybe we ought to get some doctor for her."

Fox returned with the White Bead. They were about the same age. She was a shy little girl. Now they all sat down to eat. After eating they went around visiting. There were many campfires all over the place. People had come from all the villages around.

The next morning the initiation started in mid-morning. The people were sitting around in groups, talking, the boys were playing in the flat space before the ceremonial house. Suddenly the boys noticed that all the women and girls had disappeared, somehow, but they pretended not to be nervous. Fox was the youngest of the ten who were to be initiated. There were several who were already quite big. They were playing tag and shouting but they kept looking anxiously toward the woods. They had seen something moving about there, darting from tree to tree. The grown-up men were lolling about in small groups.

Then from inside the ceremonial house there came the boom, boom, boom of the big log drum. Suddenly a Kuksu came out of the woods. He had a big head, all feathers, and you could only see his long yellow beak sticking out through the feathers. He carried a long pole with a crook at the end, one of those long poles with which you hook down dead branches for firewood.

One of the boys yelled, "There he comes! RUN!" All the boys ran for the lake, but just as they were nearing it another Kuksu emerged from the tules. The boys veered and ran for their lives in another direction, but a third Kuksu appeared from behind a bush and barred their way. There were four Kuksus surrounding them. The Kuksus started herding the boys toward the ceremonial house. Some of the boys tried to escape, but a Kuksu would take after him. They ran fast, these Kuksus, and they tripped the boys with their long crooks. Finally, they herded all the boys into the ceremonial house.

Grizzly and Tsimmu were sitting on a hillock with Bear.

"Maybe we ought not to be here," said Grizzly. "We are strangers here."

"No, no. Stay right here. Why, everybody knows you are my brother, even if you grew up somewhere else. And I said I would adopt Tsimmu as my son, so that's all right."

Now they noticed a man walking to the top of the ceremonial house. He had a thing in his hands, it was made of two flat pieces of wood, painted with lines red and black. The bigger one was at the end of a long string, and the shorter one was tied by another string so that its pointed end just touched the upper rounded end of the first one.

"That's the *ghalimatooto,* the thunder-man," said Bear. When the man was near the smoke-hole he started whirling those flat pieces of wood around his head. They made a queer penetrating noise, like the hum of an immense bee swarm. It seemed to come from everywhere at once and at the same time from nowhere, as if that hum were suspended in the air. Sometimes the smaller pieces of wood clashed against the larger one and made a clack, clack, clack, clack sound.

Tsimmu said, "Goodness! That's enough to scare anyone! Do the boys inside there know what makes the noise?"

Bear said, "Oh, I guess some of them know. I remember my own initiation. I knew about it, but when I heard it and I was lying down on my face with the other boys, I wasn't thinking about what made the noise. It just made me feel all funny inside."

Then the drum began again, several times. In between, they could hear the voice of the chief *yomta* making an oration inside the house. It didn't take so very long. Then the boys came out, looking kind of scared and-subdued. They weren't even trying to pretend any more. The grown-up men came out of the house too, with the boys, joshing them, but gently. Most of the boys were attended by a maternal uncle. Fox Boy was holding on to the hand of Turtle Old Man. They all dispersed here and there. Now the women and girls all reappeared, coming out of individual houses, and everything went on as before. Fox Boy saw Oriole and went and joined her and they both went and sat on the shore by the side of the lake.

"Was it pretty bad?" Oriole asked. "But maybe you shouldn't tell me. Maybe they told you not to speak about it."

"Oh, no they didn't tell us not to tell. I don't think there is any secret about it. I don't mind talking to you about it because you are my cousin-sister, but maybe I wouldn't want to talk to other people—wouldn't feel like it. I dunno. No, it wasn't bad, they didn't hurt us. Some of the boys cried, but that's because they were scared, that's all.

"Well, there was one part that hurt a little. Each boy had to hold a piece of burning coal in his hand. Some of the bigger boys started to fight, and the men took the boys' hands and forced them to close the fingers on it. Some of the boys yelled and called for their mothers, but it didn't do them any good. The men didn't pay any attention, they took those boys and picked them up and threw them in the air several times. I knew it was no use crying and yelling. That coal wasn't so very hot. I winced and made a face, I guess, but I didn't cry. They only made me hold it for a moment and then they knocked it off my hand. Then they just made us lie down on our faces and whipped us lightly with bow strings, but that didn't hurt. Then a *yomta* made an oration, oh, you know, told us to be good and not break the rules."

"What rules?"

"Oh, you know, hunting rules, like being careful not to go near a sick woman before going out to hunt."

"What about fishing?"

"No, not about fishing; they didn't say anything about fishing. I think it means only deer hunting, not rabbits, or ducks. Why look, Oriole, you have seen my mother set traps for rabbits, and you have seen Doctor Loon fishing."

"Yes, but she was a doctor and made her own rules."

"And what about that deer hunt with the desert Antelopes? My mother went, and the Antelope women."

"Well, that was a different country. Probably different people have different rules."

"Whadyoumean? How can they have different rules about what's good and what's bad?"

"Oh, there you go again! Their customs are different in every place where we were last summer, just like their stories, so they have different rules. What's good in one place is bad in another."

"Do you think that?"

"Why sure, I think that!"

"I don't know. I'll ask my father."

"Better ask my aunt Antelope. She knows more than my uncle Bear. She belongs to the secret society. My uncle Bear is kind of stupid like you."

"I am NOT stupid!"

"Yes, you are! But what do you care? I like you the way you are. You'll be a good hunter, you'll build good houses, you'll be a good warrior, a fear-nothing man, as they say up north."

"I don't want to be a war-man. Sounds foolish to me. I'd rather be a good hunter; at least that's useful. You eat the meat; you don't eat the people you kill in war."

"Yes, you do in some places."

"Oh, you are kidding!"

"No, that's what I have heard. Ask Tsimmu. He says sometimes they eat the hearts of the people they have killed in a fight."

"Oh, that's different, eating just the heart. That's to make them brave like the man they have killed if he was a brave man. I can understand that."

"There you go again—and you say you are not stupid. You'll be a first class war-man, a good hunter, nothing in your head!"

"Not like Tsimmu, heh? *He* is a good hunter, and he eats the hearts of his enemies, and on top of all that, he is very very bright."

"Oh, shut up, will you. Tell me what else did they do?"

"Well, several *yomtas* came and cut us two or three times on the back with a sharp flint. Old Turtle did that to me. That's all. Just more speeches and orations by the main chief and his assistants. Then it was all over, and NOW I am a full-fledged *man*—you understand?"

"You are nothing but a silly little boy to me, my own Cousin-Brother."

"I think I'll have to beat you, Oriole, to make you respect me."

"You would have to do more than beat me—which you can't do anyhow because you are too slow to catch me. You would have to show some intelligence."

"Yes, like Tsimmu, for instance. Does he beat you, Tsimmu?"

"Oh, you are crazy!"

"No, I mean, you like him, don't you, Oriole?"

"Why, sure I do. So do you."

"But I mean you are sweet on him."

"Oh, you are crazy! No, I just like him a lot, that's all. I don't want any man; I want to be a doctor. I can't be bothered with a man." She threw a handful of grass at Fox.

"Oh, you don't know what you want!" he said.

After the initiation the Bear party stayed in the village several days and visited with their cousins. Fox, Oriole, and Tsimmu played with the White Bead and several girls and boys who had come with her family to the ceremony. Oriole became very fond of White Bead and worried because she was so pale.

"Why are you sick all the time?" she asked.

"I'm not sick at all! It's a foolish notion of my mother's. Just because I am quiet! She is a very good mother, she is a very good woman, but she makes too much noise. I don't like noise."

"You have a sweet voice when you sing, White Bead."

"Do you want me to teach you some love songs?"

"No, I don't like men."

"You don't like men? What's the matter with you? I think men are wonderful!!!"

"Well, you can have them. You can take my share. I think men are stupid."

In the evening the young people sat around in a circle, singing songs and teasing each other. They sang gambling songs, deer hunting songs, and sometimes, love songs. When they asked Tsimmu to sing the love songs of his north country he said, "I have been singing them to you all along, those *wintsimalau* songs." *Wintsimalau,* he said, means worrying. "When a man is worrying he feels like being alone, he goes out and wanders, he goes to lonely places and sings to himself. That's when he goes to the mountains and the woods and the lonely lakes and springs in the woods. That's the way he gets a *tinihowi,* and . . . and sometimes he gets a *damaagomi,* a medicine for doctors."

Fox Boy didn't like worrying songs, he said.

"What I want to know is WHY don't men sing songs for making women come? We have songs for making deer come, but suppose I want to make a girl come, not a deer."

"But, silly," Oriole said, "you are supposed to be interested in deer hunting, not in girl hunting. It's the girl who hunts you."

"I don't believe it. Is that true, Mother?"

Antelope laughed her silver laugh.

"Partly. That's the way I got your father. I saw him once when he was visiting our village and I made up my mind to get him."

Bear exploded. "YOU DID NOT! It was I who did!"

Grizzly said, "Hold on a minute, Younger Brother."

"DON'T call me younger brother!"

"All right, older brother."

"I am not your older brother. I am just as young as you are."

"All right, brother-who-is-as-old-as-I-am, but listen. You just said it was *you* who DID. Did WHAT?"

"Hunt her. Hunt this woman. Why, I used to invent all kinds of pretexts to visit that village."

"Why did you?"

"I dunno. I dunno why. I used to wonder why, myself."

Everybody burst out laughing. Bear got up, disgusted, and said he was going out to see if the rain had stopped.

When it came to story-telling, Kilelli, one of the boys who had come with White Bead's family, was a great story-teller, that one. He knew stories about giants and supernatural beings, and people with only one side to their bodies.

"Tell us a story, Kilelli," they were always asking him.

"All right," Kilelli said, "I'll tell you about the madness of Tsisnam."

. . . Marten and Weasel lived together. They were great hungers. But for a long time now they had had no luck; something was wrong, somewhere.

At that time there were some Wildcat people living not far from there, and those people had a girl for whom they were going to hold a puberty dance. Now, that girl had a strong dream one night about Marten— and Marten heard of it, and he cried, "That's what spoiled our hunting luck!"

The puberty dance lasts for ten nights, the puberty-girl spends the days alone in a small hut out in the brush. Well, on the tenth day, as they were getting ready for the dance, in the evening, Marten sneaked his way into the girl's hut and ran away with her.

Old Man Wildcat said to his wife, "Go and get that girl; it's time to start dancing." She came back. She said, "She is gone! I can't find her anywhere!!"

Everybody started searching for her. They searched for her everywhere. Her younger brother was searching for her. They searched for a month. They searched

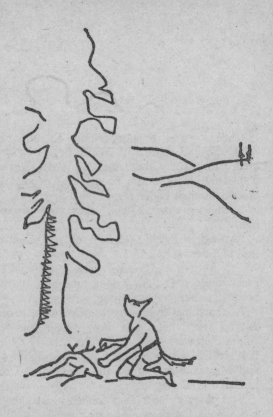

everywhere. Then they gave it up. They came back and smeared pitch on their faces and they cried. But her younger brother did not come back. He kept on searching for her. He was crying all the time. Then he went crazy.

That's when he became Tsisnam. His teeth grew long like tusks. His beard grew long. He wanted to devour people. He stuck two feathers on either side of his head and he danced. Then he started home. He got to his people's place. There was a little child playing outside.

He pounced on him and devoured him. Then he danced and shook the long feathers on either side of his head. He started to chase the children.

Somebody cried, "Water is the only thing he is afraid of." They threw water in his face. He ran off. But he came back. He lay in wait outside. He killed people and ate them. Then he danced.

His people didn't know what to do. Finally they left their home. They went to Tule Lake. They went to live on the island in the middle of the lake.

Marten had taken Wildcat Girl to his house. He put her to sleep under a rabbit-skin blanket. In the morning she peered through the strands of the blanket. She wondered where she was.

Marten went out. He gathered a lot of pine needles. He cooked them. Then he washed the girl with them from head to foot. Weasel sat watching. He didn't know what it was all about. "Where did you get that girl?" Marten paid no attention to him. He gave her some buckskin for clothes. Then he told her to stay there while he and Weasel went out hunting. Before he started he hung his porcupine-tail comb from a rafter. He said to her. "If it falls down, you will know that I am dead."

He went out and killed a deer. Another man had been stalking that deer. It was Lizard, the Terrible One, the One-Who-Had-Lost-His-Children. He was a powerful man. When Marten shot the deer, Lizard cried, "There he goes stealing my game. I'll get even with you!" And he stepped out of the brush.

"That's a big buck you've got there. How about roasting him? Let's divide him."

Marten was scared. "That's all right! You can have all of him."

Lizard skinned the deer. Then he roasted him. While he was eating the meat he kept digging out a hole, and every little while he took a look at Marten.

Marten knew that Lizard was going to challenge him. So he went a little way off into the bush and called his medicine. He changed his legs and arms into mahogany roots and manzanita roots. He twisted a long string of sinew. He tied one end to his belt and the other end to Mount Shasta. Then he went back to Lizard.

Lizard had eaten all the deer. He got up and challenged Marten to a wrestling match. He wanted to throw him into the hole he had dug. But every time he lifted him high in the air, the sinew cord twanged taut.

But the last time Lizard took a mighty heave and the cord broke. He threw Marten into the pit and covered him with burning wood. But the mahogany and manzanita arms and legs were green and did not burn well. Lizard took him out half-cooked. He carried him in one hand and started for Marten's house.

When they saw the porcupine-tail comb fall from the rafter, Weasel and Wildcat Girl knew that Marten was dead. She guessed Lizard was coming. She gave Weasel a knife and told him to stand behind the center-post. She herself took her place at the foot of the ladder.

Lizard arrived. He threw the half-cooked Marten down through the smoke-hole. Then he tried to break down the house by jumping on the roof. But he couldn't do it. Then he went down into the house.

Wildcat Girl was waiting for him. She embraced him and held him pinned against the center-post while

Weasel cut his hamstrings. He slumped to the floor. Weasel then hacked off one leg and threw it down. It made a great noise: *"Pum!"* Lizard's people way off heard it and they knew something had happened.

Weasel hacked off the other leg and threw it down. *"Pum!"*

He hacked off an arm and threw it down. *"Pum!"*

He hacked off the other arm. *"Pum!"*

Then Lizard's people started out to avenge their brother.

Tsisnam was living in the deserted winter house of his people. He was feeding on fleas. He caught them and strung them on pine needles. He was singing like a child, *"Lelu, lelu, lelu, lelu. . . ."* Then he stripped them into his mouth and chewed them with a smacking of the lips: *"tshut-tshu-tshu-tshu-tshu. . . ."* When he heard the first *"Pum!"* he paid no attention. He paid no attention to the second *"Pum!"* The last *"Pum!"* was so loud that it made him jump. He ran out of the house. He smelled the air, sniffing for people. He was hungry for people to eat.

The Lizard people were on their way to avenge their brother. But Wildcat Girl was ready for them. She had just had a child. She suckled him and put him aside. Then she told Weasel to run away. She could shift for herself.

She hid under some trash. The Lizards came. They couldn't find her but they wrecked the house.

Wildcat Girl had changed herself into a bird. She flew out from under the wreck of the house with her baby. The Lizards ran after her. She lit far off and suckled her child. When the Lizards were near, she changed herself into a thistle and the wind carried her toward her old home. Then she changed back into Wildcat Girl. She ran toward the smoke-hole of the house. The Lizards were running behind her and getting close. She met Tsisnam coming out. She cried to him, "Run for your life! They are coming after me!" He laughed and repeated, "Run for your life, they are coming after me!" She rushed down into the house. Tsisnam met the first Lizard and ate him. The other Lizards cried, "Tsisnam! Tsisnam! It's Tsisnam! Save yourselves!" They ran in all directions. Tsisnam was after them. He caught them all. He devoured them all. Then he went back to the house.

His sister had gathered all the baskets she could find. She soaked them tight and filled them with water. Then she gathered firewood and she sat with her child with the baskets of water all around her Tsisnam came down into the house. She cried to him, "I am your sister! Don't you know me?" He answered, "I am your sister! Don't you know me?" She cried, "I am the one that you cried so much about, and you went crazy because of it. Don't you know me?" But he only repeated her back and sat against the wall, glowering. She suckled her baby. He said, "I want to eat that child!" "No, you mustn't do that. That's your own nephew. I am your sister. Don't you know me? I am the one that Marten took away. You cried so much for me that you went crazy!" Then Tsisnam looked at her very hard and he almost remembered. Then he tried to grab the child again. She threw water in his face. He jumped back, and sat against the wall.

The firewood was getting low. She told him to go out and kill some more Lizards. While he was hunting for them she gathered some firewood quickly. Then he came back into the house and tried once more to grab the baby. All night long she had to keep him off by throwing water in his face. In the morning she made up her mind that she would have to get rid of him. She must get help from her people.

She had to leave the baby in his care but she put it in a basket of water.

She went to her people where they lived on the island in the middle of the lake. She asked them to lend her a boat and be ready themselves. They suspected a trap. But at last she convinced them.

While she was gone Tsisnam sat watching the baby. He was hungry for it. He commenced to lick its toes. Then he started to chew one foot. The baby kicked and splattered water in his face. Tsisnam jumped back. Several times he tried to eat his nephew.

When his sister got back she scolded him. She said, "Why don't you go to the island? You will find plenty of people there to eat. I have a boat, I can take you there." He suspected a trap. But at last he consented.

She took a very large basket. She bade him hide in it. Then she started to sew on the lid. He wanted his head to stick out. She said, "No, they might see you!" Then he wanted his feathers to stick out. But she refused. At least his whiskers. But she refused again firmly. She sewed on the lid and she started to paddle the boat. She signalled to her people on the island to start from their side.

"Are we there yet?" he asked from inside the basket.

"Not yet, but very soon."

Her people met her halfway. They had plenty of rocks in their boat.

"Are we there now?"

"Almost."

Then she pushed the basket into the water. "You will never eat people any more!"

All the people went back to their old home. She asked them to give a feast. She was looking for Weasel. They sent out invitations all around. Lots and lots of people came. She recognized Weasel among them.

She went with Weasel to the other house and there they dug out the remains of the half-cooked Marten. Weasel took a branch of sagebrush and whipped him with it. Marten came back to life.

Tsisnam was singing at the bottom of the lake. He pulled out the feathers from the sides of his head. He pulled out his teeth. He pulled out his beard. Then he got out of the basket and swam to the shore. Now he was a person again.

His sister saw him. She said, "Now I had better go and find my baby if my brother has not already eaten him." Tsisnam said nothing. He hung his head in shame. . . .

The next day Antelope spoke to her brother. "I wish you would let me take the White Bead back with us for a visit. She and Oriole get along so well."

"Yes, I think it's a very good idea. She needs a change of air. She needs to get away from her mother. She isn't sick at all, she is just growing up, that's all. Her mother is always worrying. She has a notion that somebody has poisoned the child, so she called in a medicine man, a regular *qoobakiyalxale*. He came with his bag of tricks and his rattles and his dried spiders and his dried lizards and all the rigamarole. That's all nonsense and dead stuff."

"Why didn't you doctor her, yourself? You are a *maru*."

"I am *not* a *maru*. Where did you get that idea? One does not doctor his own child. Besides, the White Bead is not sick."

"Will her mother let her go away?"

"Sure, she will. Anyhow, I can easily persuade her. I'll tell her that your brother-in-law, Grizzly, is a northern doctor."

Antelope laughed.

"You might not be so far wrong at that, Brother. He might be a doctor for all I know. He is a strange man, he keeps so much to himself, and I think he is a sad man."

"Why? He jokes and teases enough."

"Yes, but it's on the surface. He teases me to be polite because I am his sister-in-law, and he really likes to tease his own brother, but you don't see him playing much with anybody else. It's funny that he never mentions his woman. Maybe he never had one, maybe she wasn't a woman at all. I shouldn't be surprised." She laughed again. "Well, I'll have to inform Mr. Grizzly that he has been appointed medicine-man."

Tsimmu had become great friends with Kilelli, the easterner who was such a good story teller. Kilelli said, "I would like to go with you when you go back north to your own country."

"Well, come along and spend the winter with us here. I'll ask Antelope. If we were in my own country, I wouldn't have to ask her. One man more or less doesn't make any difference when there are fifty or sixty people living together in one winter-hall. But here I don't know the customs."

Antelope said, "Why, of course, certainly. I never heard of people not having room for friends of their friends!!"

The weather had become cloudy and the wind had turned to the south. Bear said, "It smells like rain to me. We had better get ready, pack, and go home." So they all got started. They were going north by the side of the lake. The two old men, Coyote and Turtle, were in the lead, swinging along at a fast gait. Tsimmu said, "Look at those two old men, they are a wonder, striding along like two young bucks. Fox, do you think when we are their age we will be as sprightly?"

Fox said, "Father, how old is old man Turtle?"

"Goodness, boy, I don't know! He was already an old man when I was a little boy."

"Is Grandfather Coyote older than he is?"

"I couldn't tell you that."

"Why? He belongs here."

"No, he doesn't belong here. You know that yourself. Have you forgotten how we found him sleeping in a little valley in the back of the hills?"

"Oh yes, that's right. It seems so long ago now."

"Nobody knows where Old Man Coyote belongs. We know he has been everywhere, and everybody knows him everywhere, but nobody knows where he ever came from or how old he is. He may have died several times and come back to life like the Coyote in the stories. Boy, for all we know, that old man is the same one who was there at the beginning of the world."

And so they were going along, *tras . . . tras . . . tras . . .* along the trail by the side of the lake, going north to their own village, gossiping and telling stories and singing gambling songs.

The weather held good; even after the winter solstice was past, it continued clear. Those who were weaving baskets or making fish nets and traps were working outside the house. The basket-makers soon had to move to the shade of a pine tree; the fibers were drying out too quickly, even in the weak sunshine.

But Fox and Tsimmu didn't do as much work as the others because they were always arguing about how the world was made. Tsimmu said, "Now listen to me! I say nobody made the world, they just found it already made and then they changed it to suit themselves, the first Coyote and the first Silver Fox and Annikadel, and the Cocoon Man and your Marumda and the Kuksu and all the people who had power in the old days. They just IMPROVED the world one way or another. Isn't that so, Grandfather Coyote?"

Coyote Old Man laughed.

"I don't know anything about it. Different people tell it different ways. You ask some old man who knows, like Turtle Old Man. He is a *yomta.*"

"Yes, that's right," Bear said, "he recites prayers and

formulas at ceremonies. It takes a long time to learn to be a *yomta*. This old man Turtle ought to be training some young fellow. Maybe he'll train you, Fox. He is your great-granduncle on your mother's side. Isn't it so, Antelope?"

"Yes, that's right, but why do you want Fox to be a *yomta*? This *yomta* business is all nonsense. What are these formulas for? What do they mean? The *yomta* doesn't know. They meant something long ago, in some kind of secret language, but now nobody knows what the words mean, so what's their use?"

"Why," said Bear, "you are a member of the secret society. You are a *matutsi*. Don't you know what they mean?"

"Listen, my man, if it's a secret society then why do you ask me to tell you?"

Fox cried, "Father, my mother does to you just what Oriole does to me. She always gets out of every argument by some trick."

Bear said, "Woman, you know very well that if the *yomta* doesn't say the prayers just exactly right at the tobacco-blessing ceremony, there won't be any tobacco that summer. I have seen it happen several times in my own life."

"How do you know the *yomta* didn't say the prayers right, since you are not a *yomta* yourself?"

"Because the tobacco crop failed that summer!"

Antelope and Oriole burst out in loud laughter. Bear got up. "There they are, ganging up on us again! Come on, Fox, let's go and bring in more tules."

Tsimmu and Kilelli were working on a deerskin. They had spread the hide over a log with the hair outside and were scraping away the hair with knives of black obsidian flint. Oriole and White Bead stopped by and watched them working. Oriole said, "White Bead, go and fetch a couple of knives, and we will help the boys. Ask Uncle Bear. I am sure he must have more knives."

Both girls sat on the ground and started scraping the

sides of the hide hanging from the log. Pretty soon Fox Boy joined them. He sat down by the White Bead and started plucking at the deer hairs with his own mussel-shell tweezers which he kept in his hair knot— he was growing a beard. Grizzly was passing by. He sat down a moment on his heels, looking, smiling at the youngsters scratching away at the hide, then he said, "Tsimmu and you, Kilelli, why are you not scraping off the grain of the hide? Aren't you making buckskin?"

Tsimmu answered, "No, Uncle, we want to use it for moccasins."

"Oh, I see," said Grizzly. "That's right. If you want it for moccasins you must leave the grain on." Then he got to his feet ponderously, as befitted an old man, and moved off with his peculiar swinging gait. He joined his brother who was twining willow wands into a fish-trap and sweating over the job.

The younger ones were scraping away. Nobody was speaking. They all felt rather drowsy in the heat. One of them said languidly, "Thirsty." Oriole went to the house, took a basket, went to the creek and filled it. She passed it around. When it came to Tsimmu, she poured the water, nice cool water, down his back.

When the sun went down they gathered their things together. Tsimmu gave the hide to Kilelli. "Here, Brother, rub some more brains on the flesh side, and we'll start again in the morning." Away off in the distance Oriole heard someone singing. It was the White Bead. She was singing a love song, a man-calling song.

In the twilight she was singing,

> Come, my fine buck,
> Come to your darling.
> Your loved one is calling.
> For you I am crying.

As the winter rolled along, Oriole worried about her friend, the White Bead. The girl was too quiet. Oriole tried to make Fox take an interest in her, but Fox was shocked.

"Why, Oriole, are you crazy? Do you forget that she is my cousin? I could never have her for my woman. It's against all the rules. I like her, I have always liked her—we were brought up together—but I mustn't ever let myself get attached to her in any other way. But I'll tell you what, that easterner, that Kilelli, I think he is interested in her."

Oriole laughed.

"Fox, sometimes I think you are not very bright. That Kilelli is interested in ME, not in the White Bead."

Fox said, "Well, what a fool I was! And are you interested in him?"

"No, I am not interested in any man. You know it."

"Not even in Tsimmu?"

"Fox, I've told you many times that I am very, very fond of Tsimmu, I admire him because he uses his brain, and he is wise, and he is courageous, and he has a good *tinihowi*. . . ."

Fox interrupted, "Yes, a good *tinihowi*, but not a good *damaagomi*, and a *damaagomi* is all *you* are interested in."

Oriole shrugged her shoulders.

"Maybe. Put it that way if you like. I just am not interested in men. Not that way."

Fox said, "I don't believe it."

Finally, one spring day, Bear decided that it was time to start on the trip north. Fox and Oriole whooped with joy, and everybody went to work with vim, cleaning the house and arranging the packs, the rabbit-skin blankets, the acorn flour, jerked meat, cooking baskets and small new baskets that they had made for presents to friends.

On the first evening they reached the same camping place under the spreading pine trees where they had camped on their other trip which now seemed so long ago. Now Fox was quite ready to go rabbit-hunting for their supper; in fact, all the youngsters went hunting, leaving Grizzly and Bear and Coyote Old Man to help Antelope gather firewood and cook enough mush for this big crowd of people.

After supper Bear addressed the people of the place as usual, the coyotes in the brush and the wolves in the woods, the rattlesnakes, the night owls, the pines, the ground, the grass, the water of the spring and the whirligigs in the spring; all the people of the place.

"We are people traveling peacefully. Our intentions are good. We have no evil in our minds. We trust you will give us protection in the night."

Fox, Oriole, and White Bead were sharing the same rabbit-skin blanket, Kilelli and Tsimmu were under another blanket, and Coyote Old Man and Grizzly made their bed together, but both were such hardened veterans of traveling that they did not bother to spread a blanket over themselves. Fox, remembering the first trip, giggled.

"Oriole, I was so green on that trip that I thought the moon was going to bed too, although it was just getting up in the sky."

Oriole was always a very late sleeper. During the night she saw Kilelli get up silently and as silently walk away from the camp and disappear into the woods. Oriole was curious, for he was not interested in hunting. "You certainly can go through the woods as quietly as the best hunter," she thought. "I could not do better myself, I who was reared in the woods. And what are you hunting for, you who say you know nothing of medicine? You are a strange one, Kilelli, the White One, and a very unhappy boy. But that is none of my affair."

Oriole could not sleep either. She was used to wandering around at night. She took the necklace of abalone pearls from under her skirt and put it around her neck, then she slipped out of camp and into the moonlit glade in which the others were asleep. She wandered aimlessly for a while, then it seemed to her that she heard someone singing. Now she could see him standing on top of a hillock, Kilelli, the White One. She thought, "Yes, you are a strange one. And for whom do you think you are singing, you who are not a hunter!" She laughed and went back to the camp.

The dawn spread out of the east slowly, coming over the tree tops and through the woods like swarms of invisible beings. In the camp they all were stretching and yawning under their blankets and singing to their shadows. But Kilelli had been up before anyone else, he had built up the campfire and now he was sitting before it warming his hands.

Fox called to him in banter, "Hey you, the White One, you must be full of power that you don't have to call your shadow like us common people."

Kilelli laughed. "Don't worry. My shadow is right near me."

Oriole said maliciously, "He is so afraid of losing his shadow that he sings to it all night long."

Kilelli did not answer, but she saw that he was looking at her from under his eyebrows. He turned his head away and said, "What can I do in a strange land? If only I had a good necklace of magic beads to protect me...."

Now it was Oriole's time to pretend she had not heard. She said, "Come, White Bead, let's go to the spring to wash." They went. Tsimmu was chuckling to himself with the rabbit-skin blanket over his head. Fox asked him, "What's the matter with you, now? Everybody seems to have some kind of secret thought this morning."

Tsimmu said, "Nothing, nothing, Fox, only this fellow Kilelli, he is an easterner but he surely acts just like us northerners. In fact, this morning this camp sounds just like a camp of my own people, with everybody shouting as they go in a gambling game. Oh, Fox, it's good to be on our way north to the land of the wild ones. It's very nice in the land of your people, all safe and orderly, with good dances and prayer formulas and the sacred tobacco plant, but nothing ever happens. There are no wild ones. The wild ones seem to be dead—dead or caught in a trap!"

Bear called, "Hey, you two, get up and come and

eat. What do you think you are, a couple of chiefs holding a palaver?"

Soon they were on the trail again, *tras . . . tras . . . tras. . . .* It was late in the afternoon when they arrived at the village of the Hawk people.

"Hawk Chief! Hawk Chief!"

"Well, WHAT do you want? Can't you find the door? Are you blind?"

"You must not talk that way!" said the older one of the Hawk Chiefs to his brother. "Why are you so rough? How do you know but that these are friends come to visit us? Come in! come in! The door is on the east side. Use the big door, not the little one. Why, these are our old friends who passed this way before! And with them is Old Man Coyote himself. And here is the little boy who wanted to keep our Chief for a pet. Now he is a young warrior. And who is this little one, this little girl who just crawled in through the Chief's own little door? Is she the one who was a baby wrapped in a pack basket? Older Chief, older Chief, you Wiwwa Wek-Wek, they have brought a wife for you."

The Hawk people roared with laughter, but the older

Hawk Chief, who was the Sparrow Hawk, was mad. He went out through his own door and they heard him singing his war song outside in the night. *"Ya'ya-henna. . . ."*

The next morning the Bear party made their departure, but before they went they made presents; they gave some of the beautiful little baskets decorated with feathers and other presents.

The Hawk Chief had taken Kilelli aside.

"I like the way you played handgame last night. I like the way you sang. Here are some beads for you. They are a special kind, there is power in them. Keep them hidden, keep them in your hair, in your topknot. Don't show them to people. Sometime you may be in trouble, then they will help you. I liked the way you played handgame last night, the way you sang. That was good, that was good indeed."

Soon they were on the trail again, they were traveling along a valley. Fox said, "Mother, do you remember the last trip through here, and how we stopped at this same village of Hawks, and then we had an argument, Grandfather Coyote, you and I?"

"No, it wasn't here, boy. It was later on the trip. You have either forgotten or you are all mixed up. Grandfather was not with us when we visited the village of the Hawks. We did not go to his house till later on the trip. But I think I know what you mean. It was after Grandfather Coyote told us that same story about the Hawk Chief of the old days that you started the argument with him and me."

Oriole said, "Aunt Antelope, do you mean to tell me

213

that Fox was already in the habit of arguing when he was a little boy?"

Antelope laughed. "Yes, he was always that way."

Kilelli asked, "What was the argument about?"

"Oh, it was about how could people be people and not be people at the same time. When Grandfather Coyote said, 'That's the end of the tale,' Fox said, 'Why, NO, Grandfather! the story is not finished. Your great-great-grandfather stopped the fire, and then he stopped the flood, and then he got new fire from the people in the South World, and then he got the Sun so as to have light to see by. But still there are no people in the world!' Then I said, 'What do you mean, there are no people in the world? Isn't Hawk people? Isn't Dove people? and Rat, and Flint, and all the rest?' But he wasn't satisfied, he kept insisting that they were people, all right, and yet they were not people."

Tsimmu looked at Kilelli.

"What are you laughing about, you White One?"

"Nothing, nothing. Oh, well, just that the same question has always bothered me too."

White Bead asked, "What do YOU think, you Tsimmu?"

"I? Oh, I don't think anything. I am a WOLF!"

"That's no answer!" said Oriole.

Fox laughed.

"You can't trap that wild owl. Eh, you, give me that baby, she is too heavy for you." And he swung the Quail on his shoulders, astride his pack.

They went on along the valley, *tras . . . tras . . . tras.* Fox said, "All right, go on laughing. We will soon arrive at the village of the Flints, and then we'll see what you say about it. Are they people, are they not people?"

Kilelli asked, "Do you mean we are coming to a village where the people are real supernatural beings?"

Oriole asked, "What do YOU know about it?"

He answered, "Not so much as you do!"

Everybody laughed. Tsimmu shouted, "He wins!! Throw the bones across."

The Bear party now came to somewhat rougher country. Finally, they reached a secluded valley in the hills.

"FLINT Chief! FLINT Chief!"

The Flint people came swarming out of their house, jostling and clinking.

"Well! Here are our friends again. Here are our visitors again!"

While the whole Bear party went down the smoke-hole ladder, Kilelli separated himself from the others and went off by himself. Nobody noticed that he was gone—nobody except Oriole.

It was not long before the drum was beating inside the ceremonial house of the Flints. Boom, BOOM, boom, boom, BOOM, boom. The people were getting ready; they were playing, joshing, getting into fantastic costumes, getting ready for the game.

"Well, Mrs. Antelope! Here you are, but where is that baby? and that little Fox? Why, there he is, now a grown man, a hunter! And how come you have Grandfather Coyote with you? We haven't seen him for ages and ages, we had come to think you didn't exist any more!"

"Ho, ho, ho! You never can kill us Coyotes! We live forever."

Inside the ceremonial house there was great bustle and joshing and teasing. The Bear party were mixing with the Flints, trying on costumes and feather head-dresses.

"Oh, you Flint! Don't jostle against me! You are cutting me to pieces with your sharp edges."

The game started and they were swinging and sway-ing in the rhythm, the Bear players on this side and the Flints on the other. They were swaying their bodies from the middle up in time with the song, and the eyes shining in the dark and watching. Song after song, and the rhythm changed. They shouted "HA!" and they showed the bones. "Throw them across, throw them across. Pay us a counter! Pay us a counter."

An old Flint man in the rear said, "Good singers! Good singers on both sides! I would not know where to bet."

The gambling went on. It was now past the middle of the night, the bones were sometimes all but one, the last one, on one side, and then the luck would turn to the other side. And then, suddenly, there was a stir. Somebody had come into the ceremonial house, some-body was standing there in the shadows. Oriole was aware of him immediately, but no one else. He slipped into the game amidst the singing and shouting. He slipped in among the Flints and there he was, singing and swaying with the rhythm. Now he was shouting with them, and he was shooting right, he was shooting straight. "Oh, you Kilelli, you the White One, why are you on the wrong side? Because I wouldn't have you?"

The game went on and on with no side winning. Everybody was tired and secretly wishing to give up. An old Flint man made as if to go up and put his foot square in the middle of the fire.

"Hey, you old chief! Look what you have done, you have scattered the counters!" "Let's give up, fellows, It's late. I'm tired." "I also. I'm tired! Let's quit!"

Everybody was looking for a place to make his bed, spreading blankets in the moonlight, laughing and giggling. "Here! that's my blanket!" "You don't need a blanket, you have a partner!" "Go to bed! Go to bed, young fellow!" "Let's make a fire here, a small one." "I wouldn't share a bed with a Flint! Their limbs are too sharp!" "Bah! what are you talking about? That was a long time ago!" "Go to bed, go to bed, young ones. Let us sleep!" And in the shadows there were giggles.

Oriole was sleeping away out by herself, as usual when there was a crowd. She did not like crowds. Now she saw a shadow settle on the ground near her blanket.

"What do you want, White One?"

"I do not know," and the shadow melted away again into the dark woods under the moonlight.

There was now silence over the camp. Antelope propped herself on one elbow and listened to the night. Bear was snoring. "Is that Tsimmu over there? He is probably somewhere with a Flint girl."

Oriole said to the night, "I will never join with you, White One. Go your own unhappy way!" The camp was now quiet. She gathered her blanket and went over and crawled in with Fox and the White Bead.

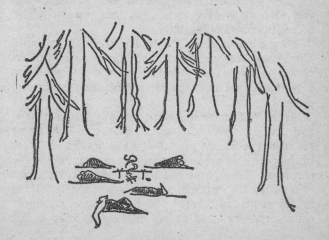

The Bear party was on the trail again, and what a party! How different from that time before when only Bear, Antelope, and little Fox Boy had left their home to visit the Crane people. Then the Quail was only a baby strapped in a cradle-board, and now she was a little girl almost, sometimes walking with her hand in someone else's, or strapped in the sitting-up basket on Antelope's back, facing backward and smiling to the next person in the line. She was a happy child and she laughed when you made faces at her. When Coyote Old Man made as if to bite her toes, she kicked his face with shrieks of laughter.

They climbed along the trail between the rounded hills. They were getting into that lonely country of secluded valleys where they had found old Grandfather Coyote sleeping away the years in his little house with no door.

At the end of the line were the stragglers, Antelope and the little Quail, Coyote Old Man, and Bear under his always enormous pack. But it was not the heaviness of the pack that made Bear the last in line; he was the shepherd. Although he had none of the accoutrements of a chief—for instance, poor Bear was totally lacking in the ability to "orate"—he had the real qualities: calm, prudence, and above all, responsibility to his group. They were traveling through strange country, and Bear saw to it that no one was left behind.

The White Bead was often with Antelope to whom she was devoted. Oriole was hardly ever on the line of march. She was an inveterate "side-tripper," forever going off alone on voyages of discovery. This worried Antelope and Bear, but no one could cope with Oriole's independence or her love of lonely, wild places.

Both girls carried fairly good packs, although, of course, not as heavy as those of the boys. And their tump lines did not pass over the forehead but over the chest, just above the breasts. Their loads were light enough to be taken off easily over the head. The boys had to sit down in front of the pack on a rock, slip the tump line over the forehead, and then get up with a grunt. Once under the pack, if the trail was not too steep, they preferred to go fast, at a sort of dog-trot, with short steps, and the knees never completely unbent. Grizzly was always a mile or two ahead, going slowly. He was the best traveler of them all. He was always the first to start, while the boys were likely to be the last. Sometimes they let everybody get far ahead, and then those three passed everybody on the run in that kind of dog-trot that suited them best.

Now as the boys climbed a hill they could see Grizzly, who had stopped on the divide, looking down into the valley on the other side. When they caught up with him, he pointed out to them a small house standing in the center of the little valley below, a small valley with a stream running through it under the sycamores and alders. There was also a big redwood tree. And *smoke curled upward from the smoke-hole* of that little house.

Fox said, "I am not sure, but I think that's Grandfather Coyote's house. I might be mistaken, it was a long time ago when we came through here and found Grandfather Coyote asleep in his house. Yes, this looks exactly like the place."

The girls arrived soon, and at last Coyote Old Man, Bear, and Antelope. They were all somewhat disturbed at finding Grandfather Coyote's house purloined by someone—all, that is, except Old Man Coyote himself, who never was disturbed by anything. He chuckled.

"I think I have an idea who is in there!" But he would not say any more.

They went down into the little valley with the house in the middle. There was no sign of life around the house, except the smoke that was curling upward out of the smoke-hole. Old Man Coyote called. He called and called again. Then from the inside somebody answered, "The door is on the roof. Can't you see the ladder sticking out? You must be blind!"

Coyote Old Man was chuckling and chuckling.

"That's my elder brother, Coyote of the South World. He is a rough fellow, but he's all right."

Bear, Antelope, and all the rest were amazed, but they followed Coyote up the roof and down the center-post ladder. It was a small house and there was just enough room for them to sit around the wall. For a while nobody spoke, then Grandfather Coyote from the North World said *"Yo Sume'e,* elder brother from the South World. Welcome. Are things well in your place? Are the people healthy? Are they behaving themselves?"

"Yo Sume'e. Yes, everything is well with us. The people are behaving themselves. They follow our plan. They are peaceful. I have not had to destroy them for a long time. So I came to visit you. I came to see if my younger brother needed my help."

"Thank you, elder brother, thank you. I have been on a tour of inspection because I have learned that you cannot go to sleep for more than forty winks before the people are up to their old tricks and misbehaving again. I am glad I came through this place and found you. Now you can join me on our tour of inspection. *Yo Sume'e."*

Now the Coyote from the North World took the little buckskin sack hanging from his neck and poked the end of his straight wooden pipe out of the sack. He grabbed the end and pulled and pulled it and pulled it all out. It was at least two feet long, and there were figures carved on it, figures of lakes, trees, rivers, animals, and people. Fox whispered to Oriole, "See, you never would believe."

Coyote now smoked. Meanwhile, the Coyote from the South World also had pulled his pipe out of the little buckskin sack hanging from his neck. And now he smoked. Then they both got up and turned around each other four times, just as they tell in the stories. Then they exchanged pipes. They said *"Yo Sume'e!* We will have a good journey; enemies will not attack us from ambush; we will not fall sick by the wayside; we will find our old friends, and we will make new friends. *Yo Sume'e!* Thus it will be, *nin 'ikba'e."* They turned around each other again four times the opposite way, and then they exchanged pipes once more.

The Bear party spent the rest of that day in camp, repairing their footgear and packing outfits, tump lines and nets, and telling stories. Those people were never tired of hearing the same stories over and over again. Some of them, like Kilelli, could tell a story with great artistry. Others, like the White Bead, were bashful and mumbled and got tangled up. The new Coyote turned out to be as good as the Coyote from the North. It was very hard to tell them apart, but Fox noticed that the South Coyote had a kink in his tail.

The Coyote said, "Why, I never knew I had a kink in my tail. You never told me, younger brother."

"I never noticed it myself. This fellow never misses a trick!"

Somewhere away back in these lonely hills, so said Old Man Coyote, was the Weasel's house. In one of the little spit-and-scratch exchanges between Kilelli and Oriole, she taunted him.

"You are always looking for a power, for a *tinihowi*. Well, here is your chance. Go and look for Weasel's house. Maybe you'll find him there; maybe you can get him for a power."

And now Kilelli was not in the line of march. He had skipped off somewhere without telling anyone. And Oriole was sorry and blamed herself. But Tsimmu said, "Don't worry. The Gilak hasn't stolen him. Besides, how do you expect him to get anywhere unless he is ready to take a chance."

"Would you take a chance, Tsimmu?"

"Certainly not! I am a hunter, not a doctor. As for hunting, I told you I have my *tinihowi,* that Wolf."

And so Kilelli had left the others and gone searching. *Intsimalao* they call it. Well, it wasn't really *intsimalao* but on the edge of it, on the border of it. When you are *intsimalao* you are nearly crazy. You go wandering, you are worried, lonely, sad . . . you don't know what's the matter with you. Kilelli hadn't reached that stage yet, but he was not very far from it. He had left the party and climbed several ridges, but still going in the same general direction. He knew he would find their camp that evening, even if late. It was not the

first time he had traveled through wild country; he was not afraid and he was determined to show Oriole that he could face Weasel! And now he found a house, back in there, and how lonesome it looked in a fold of the hills!

Kilelli entered the house. There was no one inside. The sunshine came in at the smoke-hole and made the smoke from the fire go up in lazy blue curls. Occasionally the fire gave a crackle, but otherwise the house was silent. "It must be Weasel's house," Kilelli thought. When he had gone in nobody had given him the traditional joking welcome, "The door is on the north side. Can't you see it? You must be blind." Kilelli felt uneasy. He did not go poking around with curiosity like the old-time Weasel of the stories. He dropped his pack on the ground in front of the fire and sat on it. He wished he had not come—just to show that girl, Oriole!

The Center Post spoke. "Someone came in, and it's not our father."

The Main Rafter said, "When our father comes home he will challenge this young man to a gambling match and shoot him; then we will have fresh meat."

The Fire said, "That's right. I haven't roasted any deer meat for a long time."

The Door Jamb said, "I feel sorry for this young man. He must be a brave man to go around challenging in strangers' houses. I always had a liking for a man with courage."

The Ladder said, "Me too! And our father also. You know how soft-hearted he can be with a young man who goes wandering, looking for power."

Kilelli spoke up. "Say, WHOSE house is this anyhow? Isn't this Weasel's house? I thought it was Weasel's house."

At this the Center Post, the Center Post Ladder, the Fire, the Main Rafter, the Long Rafter, the Rafter-over-the-Doorway, the Door Jamb, they all let out shrieks of laughter.

"Weasel's house? Ha, ha, ha, listen to him. Weasel's house, ha, ha, ha! Weasel indeed! That little runt, that *dinnike!* Who is afraid of him?"

"Well, WHOSE house is it, then?"

But now there was silence in the house. Nobody spoke. The fire crackled, the smoke rose in thin curls. Kilelli was feeling downright uneasy; he was scared; he wished he had not come.

Now he heard a noise back of him, hosh, hosh, hosh. Kilelli knew that sound, he had heard it in the old-time stories of long ago. It was the Cho-Djo-Djo, one of the Supernatural Beings in the tales of long ago among his own people. The Cho-Djo-Djo has only *one half* to his body.

Kilelli turned around sharply but he saw no one. And now he heard it again, hosh, hosh, hosh; this time it came from the other side of the house, hosh, hosh, hosh. It came from behind the center-post, from a crack in the door jamb. Kilelli grabbed his pack by the tump line and started to run, but the Cho-Djo-Djo stood in front of him and barred his way.

"Is that how a visitor behaves? Is that the way you people behave? I thought you had come to challenge my power! I am disappointed!"

"I *have* come to challenge your power, but not to play silly games of hide-and-seek!" shouted Kilelli.

"Now, that's the way to talk! That's the way I like a young man to talk. All right, we'll have a game, but I warn you I don't play for fun, like children. I shoot to kill. Are you ready? You are the visitor, so you have the right to shoot first."

Now the Cho-Djo-Djo took the bones, and Kilelli started to guess. Now he is thinking hard. He strings the arrow. He pulls it back to the head. He takes careful aim. He lets go. The arrow went straight and true, but *there was nothing there,* only empty air! The Supernatural Being at the last moment had shifted himself to the other half of his body. Kilelli thought bitterly, "Scoundrel! What a trick! Now I am lost, indeed. I wish I had not come here just because a silly girl taunted me."

Now it was the turn of the Cho-Djo-Djo to shoot. He killed Kilelli at the first shot. Kilelli tumbled forward into the fire.

Now, the Fire said, "That was a brave young fellow."

The Door Jamb said, "Maybe he was looking for supernatural power and maybe he was looking for a spirit protector."

The Center Post Ladder said, "Center Post, Older Brother, what do you think of it? Do you think it was a nice thing for our father to do?"

The Cho-Djo-Djo stood there silent for a while, then he picked up the body of Kilelli and he whipped him with the bow-string, and Kilelli came back to life. The Cho-Djo-Djo sat him on his pack and he said, "I took pity on you. You needed a lesson, you are too cocky. All right, I'll watch for you. You are going into a country of old-time doctors, not the half-dead fellows of our land with their silly mumbo-jumbo. These doctors where you are going, the country is full of them—mean ones—so watch your step. I'll help you. When you are in trouble, sing my song and I will come. I am not afraid of these northerners, I'll enjoy matching myself against them."

Suddenly Kilelli woke up. He was lying with his head on top of his pack. He was laying on top of a ridge, and the sun was halfway down. There was no house of any kind.

Kilelli got up. He picked up his pack and adjusted the tump line. Now he was jog-trotting along the ridge, going fast to catch up with the Bear party.

Fox Boy and Oriole were sitting by the side of the lake.

Oriole said, "Fox, WHAT did you DO to your tail."

"What's the matter with it?" asked Fox in an injured tone.

"Why, it's so ragged—and it's getting shorter and shorter . . . ever since you were initiated."

"Oh, go on with you," said Fox, trying to bring the end of his tail to the front to look at it. He was turning and turning around. He finally got dizzy and sat down, and Oriole burst into loud laughter.

"You had better not laugh, Miss. I didn't want to say anything about it, but *your* wings have been getting shorter and kind of ragged. I have been noticing it."

"Oh, *have* you, little boy? Well, let me tell you, we don't call these *wings* any more. That's just an old-fashioned word. These are *arms*. Arms, not wings, you understand? ARMS. Say a-r-m-s."

"I don't want to, I DON'T WANT TO. I don't want to be a *Man;* I want to be a Fox."

"Oh, the HA-HAS again. You are reverting."

Fox was laughing. He said, "Seriously, Oriole, why did we grow up so fast? Only yesterday, when we began our story and I started to see the world with my father, who was then a real Bear. . . ."

Oriole interrupted. "No, you are mistaken. He was not a real Bear yet, he was only a beginning of a bear, he was a person-bear. Now he is a bearman—I mean a man-bear . . . I mean . . ."

"Oh, keep quiet. You are getting me all mixed up again."

"No, Fox, listen to me; I will explain. The man who is telling our story, it's his fault, he has done something wrong with the machinery of time, he has let it go too fast. You see, he was supposed to take a million years to tell our story. The poor fellow, he is too old, he gets all mixed up. He should go and take a rest in the country for a while."

"Oh, my, my, my!" sighed Fox, "the only thing to do is to start again RIGHT AT THE BEGINNING." Fox looked curiously at Oriole. "What do you mean, a MILLION years?"

"Why, I mean an infinity of time, just as Tsimmu was telling in *his* story of the creation of the world. Don't you remember? Ten times ten times ten times ten years, *molossi molossi molossi tellim piduuwi.* When Cocoon Man was floating around in nothing but air and fog he waited a million years for that cloud to come near enough so he could jump on it."

"Yes," said Fox. "Yes, just like Marum'da, who made the world and then he went to sleep. That's an infinity of time, but it must stop somewhere—it can't go on forever. It must stop somewhere."

Oriole asked, "WHY?"

Fox thought a moment then he said, "I dunno. But listen, Oriole, what's time anyway?"

Oriole said, "Why, it's ten times ten times ten times ten years. What else do you want it to be?"

Fox said, "I dunno. I guess it's growing old."

Oriole said, "All right, then, some people grow old faster than others. You know that yourself. Just as some people walk faster than others; it all depends on who is looking at it."

"Why, Oriole, you are crazy. It depends on who is walking, not on the man who is looking at the fellow who is walking."

"No, certainly NOT. Look at that man over there walking. He seems to be just crawling along, but if you were close to him, he would be going much faster. That's the way with the man who is telling this story. Sometimes he is closer and sometimes he is farther away, so for him that makes us go faster or slower."

Fox said, "Oriole, you drive me crazy. Now I don't know whether I am standing on my head or my feet. It's like that time when we first met you and your father."

"Listen, Fox, it is not I who started this idea that there was a man telling this story, it was you. For all we know, there is no such man."

"Of course, there is not. I invented him."

"That doesn't prove anything. Marum'da invented the people, and they existed whether he liked it or not. Maybe you invented the man who is telling this story, so now he exists. It's too bad, but now you can't get rid of him."

"Yes, I will. I'll destroy him the way Marum'da did the people."

"Then you know what will happen, Mister? You won't exist any more, because he is the one who is telling the story."

"Oh, oh, oh, stop, Oriole!" Fox was holding his head in both hands. Then he laughed as he pulled Oriole to her feet and they both ran down the hill.

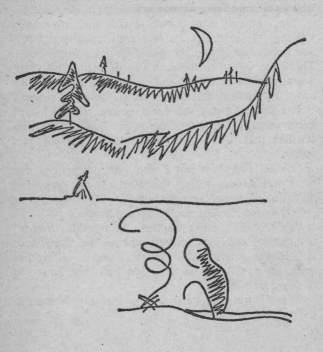

APPENDIX

INDIAN RELIGION

The Coyote stories form a regular cycle, a saga. This is true of all of California; and it extends eastward even as far as the Pueblos of Arizona and New Mexico. Coyote has a double personality. He is at once the Creator and the Fool. This antinomy is very important. Unless you understand it you will miss the Indian psychology completely—at least you will miss the significance of their literature (because I call their tales, their "old-time stories," literature).

The wise man and the buffoon: the two aspects of Coyote, Coyote Old Man. Note that I don't call them the good and the evil, because that conception of morality does not seem to play much part in the Pit River attitude to life. Their mores are not much concerned with good and evil. You have a definite attitude toward moral right and moral wrong. I don't think the Pit River has. At least, if he has, he does not try to coerce. I have heard Indians say: "That's not right what he is doing, that fellow. . . ." "What d'you mean it's not right?" "Well . . . you ain't supposed to do things that way . . . it never was done that way . . . there'll be trouble." "Then why don't you stop him?" "Stop him? How can I stop him? It's his way."

The Pit Rivers (except the younger ones who have gone to the Government school at Fort Bidwell) don't ever seem to get a very clear conception of what you mean by the term God. This is true even of those who speak American fluently, like Wild Bill. He said to me: "What is this thing that the white people call God? They are always

The material that follows is excerpted from Mr. de Angulo's "Indians in Overalls," published in *The Hudson Review,* Vol. III, No. 3, Autumn, 1950. Copyright, 1950, by *The Hudson Review.*

talking about it. It's goddam this and goddam that, and in the name of the god, and the god made the world. Who is that god, Doc? They say that Coyote is the Indian God, but if I say to them that God is Coyote, they get mad at me. Why?"

"Listen, Bill, tell me . . . do the Indians think, really think, that Coyote made the world? I mean, do they really think so? Do you really think so?"

"Why of course I do. . . . Why not? . . . Anyway . . . that's what the old people always said . . . only they don't all tell the same story. Here is one way I heard it: it seems like there was nothing everywhere but a kind of fog. Fog and water mixed, they say, no land anywhere, and this here Silver Fox . . ."

"You mean Coyote?"

"No, no, I mean Silver Fox. Coyote comes later. You'll see, but right now, somewhere in the fog, they say, Silver Fox was wandering and feeling lonely. *Tsikuellaaduwi maandza tsikualaasa.* He was feeling lonely, the Silver Fox. I wish I would meet someone, he said to himself, the Silver Fox did. He was walking along in the fog. He met Coyote. 'I thought I was going to meet someone,' he said. The Coyote looked at him, but he didn't say anything. 'Where are you traveling?' says Fox. 'But where are you traveling? Why do you travel like that?' 'Because I am worried.' 'I also am wandering,' said the Coyote; 'I also am worrying and traveling.' 'I thought I would meet someone, I thought I would meet someone. Let's you and I travel together. It's better for two people to be traveling together, that's what they always say. . . .' "

"Wait a minute, Bill. . . . Who said that?"

"The Fox said that. I don't know who he meant when he said *that's what they always say.* It's funny, isn't it? How could he talk about other people since there had never been anybody before? I don't know. . . . I wonder about that sometimes, myself. I have asked some of the old people and they say: That's what I have been wondering myself, but that's the way we have always heard it told. And then you hear the Paiutes tell it different! And our own people down the river, they also tell it a little bit different from us. Doc, maybe the whole thing just never happened. . . . And maybe it did happen but everybody tells it different. People often do that, you know. . . ."

"Well, go on with the story. You said that Fox had met Coyote. . . ."

"Oh, yah. . . . Well, this Coyote he says: 'What are we going to do now?' 'What do you think?' says Fox. 'I don't know,' says Coyote. 'Well then,' says Fox, 'I'll tell you: LET'S MAKE THE WORLD.' 'And how are we going to do that?' 'WE WILL SING,' says the Fox.

"So, there they were singing up there in the sky. They were singing and stomping and dancing around each other in a circle. Then the Fox he thought in his mind: CLUMP OF SOD, come!! That's the way he made it come: *by thinking.* Pretty soon he had it in his hands. And he was singing, all the while he had it in his hands. They were both singing and stomping. All of a sudden the Fox threw that clump of sod, that *tsapettia,* he threw it down into the clouds. 'Don't look down!' he said to the Coyote. 'Keep on singing! Shut your eyes, and keep them shut until I tell you.' So they kept on singing and stomping around each other in a circle for quite a while. Then the Fox said to the Coyote: 'Now, look down there. What do you see?' 'I see something . . . I see something . . . but I don't know what it is.' 'All right. Shut your eyes again!' Now they started singing and stomping again, and the Fox thought and wished: Stretch! Stretch! 'Now look down again. What do you see?' 'Oh! It's getting bigger!' 'Shut your eyes again and don't look down!' And they went on singing and stomping up there in the sky. 'Now look down again!' 'Oooh! Now it's big enough!' said the Coyote.

"That's the way they made the wrold, Doc. Then they both jumped down on it and they stretched it some more. Then they made mountains and valleys; they made trees and rocks and everything. It took them a long time to do all that!"

"Didn't they make people, too?"

"No. Not people. Not Indians. The Indians came much later, after the world was spoiled by a crazy woman, Loon. But that's a long story. . . . I'll tell you some day."

"All right, Bill, but tell me just one thing now: there was a world now; then there were a lot of animals living on it, but there were no people then. . . ."

"Whad'you mean there were no people? Ain't animals people?"

"Yes, they are . . . but . . ."

"They are not Indians, but they are people, they are alive . . . Whad'you mean animal?"

"Well . . . how do you say 'animal' in Pit River?"

". . . I dunno. . . ."

"But suppose you wanted to say it?"

"Well . . . I guess I would say something like *teeqaade-wade toolol aakaadzi* (world-over, all living) . . . I guess that means animals, Doc."

"I don't see how, Bill. That means people, also. People are living, aren't they?"

"Sure they are! That's what I am telling you. Everything is living, even the rocks, even that bench you are sitting on. Somebody *made that bench for a purpose*, didn't he? Well then, *it's alive*, isn't it? Everything is alive. That's what we Indians believe. White people think everything is dead. . . ."

"Listen, Bill. How do you say 'people'?"

"I don't know . . . just *is*, I guess."

"I thought that meant 'Indian.'"

"Say . . . ain't we *people?!*"

"So are the whites!"

"Like hell they are!! We call them *inillaaduwi*, 'tramps,' nothing but tramps. They don't believe anything is alive. They are dead themselves. I don't call that 'people.' They are smart, but they don't know anything."

INDIAN DANCING

The principle of Indian dancing is stomping. It is not, like our own dancing, based on raising the heel and standing on the toes. On the contrary, the foot is raised flat from the ground, put down again flat, and then, as it were, pushed down into the earth by a bending at the knee. There is thus produced a combination of heaviness and spring-like ease.

A typical Indian dance lasts all night. Every hour or so, the dancers come out and perform. In between the dances the people try to keep awake. Indians appear to enjoy the lack of sleep and the effort to keep awake. It seems to serve to blend all the diverse performances of one night into a dreamlike whole.

INDIAN SPEECHMAKING

To make a speech, among Indians, requires a specialized kind of talent. A regular speech must be in stilted, archaic talk, delivered in a high, unmodulated voice, in rapid sentences broken by short silences. Only some people know how to do this.

INDIAN LUCK

It was Robert Spring who first made me understand about the *dinihowi*. "That's what we Indians call *luck*. A man has got to have luck, no matter for what, whether it's for gambling, or for hunting, for making love, for anything unless he wants to be just a common Indian . . . like me."

We were lying flat on our backs under a juniper. After a silence he started again: "When a fellow is young, everybody is after him to go to the mountains and get himself a *dinihowi*. The old men say: You'll never amount to anything if you don't go and catch a *dinihowi*. And then you hear other fellows brag about their luck at gambling, or how they got a good *dinihowi* for hunting. Well, there come a time when a young fellow starts to feel uneasy, kind of sad, kind of worried; that's just about the time he's getting to be a man grown up. Then he start to 'wander,' that's what we call it, wandering. They say: Leave him alone, he is wandering. That's the time you go to the hills, you don't come home, you stay out all night, you get scared, you cry; two, three days you go hungry. Sometime your people get worried, come after you, but you throw rocks at them: Go away, I don't want you, leave me alone. You get pretty hungry, you get dizzy, you are afraid of grizzly bears. Maybe you fall asleep and someone come wake you up, maybe a wolf, push your head with his foot, maybe bluejay peck at your face, maybe little fly get in your ear, he say: Hey! Wake up! What you doing here? Your people worrying about you! You better go home! I seen you wandering here, crying, hungry, I pity you. I like you. I help you. Listen, this is my song. Remember that song. When you want me, you come here and sing my song. I'll hear you. I'll come. . . ."

I said to Robert Spring: "But then, I don't see what is

the difference between the *dinihowi* and the *damaagome*. . . ."

"There is no difference. It's all the same. Only the *damaagome* that's for doctors."

"How does the doctor get his *damaagome?*"

"Just like you and me get a *dinihowi*. He goes to the mountain. He cries. Then someone comes and says: This is my song, I'll help you."

"Well then, I don't see any difference."

"I am telling you there is no difference. Only the *dinihowi* that's for plain Indians like you and me, and the *damaagome* that's for doctors. . . . Well, I'll tell you, there is maybe some difference. The *damaagome* is kind of mean, quarrelsome, always fighting. The *dinihowi* is more peaceful."

INDIAN MEDICINE

I had gone into that house looking for an old fellow named Blind Hall, or Johnny Hall (his name, I found out later, was Tahteumi, meaning "red trail," or "red track," or "sunset trail"). They had told me he was one of the most powerful medicine men around. But the tattooing girl said he wasn't there; this was his house, but he had gone to another camp. She said he was sick. "He was going to town the other day with his old woman; they were driving along in their old buggy; automobile come from behind; upset buggy; old Hall didn't know he was hurt, but he must have dropped his shadow; he went on to Hantiyu, but he got pretty sick; he is coming back today; he is going to doctor himself tonight."

That sounded interesting. I thought I would hang around. Maybe I would learn something. So I wandered around. About noon, Blind Hall arrived in the old rattling creaking swaying buggy with his old woman and the old old decrepit horse. I knew right away I had seen him before somewhere, sometime: that massive face, the slightless eyes, the very thick lips and quite a lot of white beard for an Indian. "Hallo, white man, I remember you, you stop once, we camp side road, you give me can beans, bacon, you eat with us, you treat me good, you all right, I remember you, I remember your voice—I am pretty sick now, dropped my shadow on the road, can't live without my shadow, maybe I die, I dunno. . . . I doctor myself tonight. You stay, you help sing tonight."

Blind Hall called his medicine "my poison." The Indian word is *damaagome*. Some Indians translate it in English as "medicine," or "power," sometimes "dog" (in the sense of pet dog, or trained dog). Blind Hall was not boastful like Sukmit; he was full of quiet dignity. As to his age, goodness knows, he said he and Jack Folsom were young men together, and once they got mad at each other: "I called him by his name and he called me by my name" (you are not supposed to call an Indian by his personal name; that's too personal, too private; you call him by his term of relationship to you—uncle, grandfather, brother-in-law, or whatever—or by his nickname).

Blind Hall was groaning and bellyaching about the pain in his ribs. We were sitting in the sun. "Give me a cigarette, white man. Mebbe I die. I dunno. That autocar he knock my shadow out of me; shadow he stay on the road now can't find me; can't live without my shadow! . . . It's too bad, mebbe I die . . . tonight I doctor myself, I ask my poisons . . . I got several poisons . . . I got Raven, he live on top mountain Wadaqtsuudzi, he know everything, watch everything. . . . I got Bullsnake, he pretty good too. . . . I got Louse, Crablouse, live with people, much friends, he tell me lots things. . . . I got Jim Lizard, he sit on rock all day, he pretty clever but not serious, he dam liar. . . . Sometime I doctor sick man, call my poisons come over my head, they fight, Raven he says that man poisoned, Bullsnake say no he not poisoned, he broke rule hunting . . . and then this here Jim Lizard he say, Oh, let's go home that man going to die anyhow! . . . Then Raven he shake his finger at him, he say: Who ask you what you think? Why don't you help our father? [The poisons call the medicine man "my father," *ittu ai*—the medicine-man calls his poison *ittu damaagome*, "my *damaagome*," or whatever you want to translate that word by: medicine, poison, power. . . .] You can go home if you want to, we will stay here and help our father. Then Jim Lizard mebbe he stay and help and mebbe he tell me lie. I can't depend on him. . . . Ohh . . . it hurt me inside here. Maybe I die. Everybody

die sometime. . . . I ask my poison tonight. You white
man, you help, you sing too. More people sing more good.
Sometime my poison very far away, not hear. Lots people
sing, he hear better."

That evening, we all gathered at sundown. Jack Steel,
an Indian from Hantiyu who usually acted as Blind Hall's
"interpreter," had arrived. He went out a little way into
the sagebrush and called the poisons. "Raven, you, my
poison, COME! (*qaq, mi', ittu damaagome, tunnoo*) . . .
Bullsnake, my poison, come. . . . Crablouse, my poison,
cooome. . . . You all, my poisons, COOOME!!" It was kind
of weird, this man out in the sagebrush calling and calling
for the poisons, just like a farmer calling his cows home.

We all gathered around the fire; some were sitting on the
ground, some were lying on their side. Blind Hall began
singing one of his medicine songs. Two or three who knew
that song well joined him. Others hummed for a while before catching on. Robert Spring said to me: "Come on,
sing. Don't be afraid. Everybody must help." At that time
I had not yet learned to sing Indian fashion. The melody
puzzled me. But I joined in, bashfully at first, then when I
realized that nobody was paying any attention to me, with
gusto.

Blind Hall had soon stopped singing, himself. He had
dropped into a sort of brown study, or as if he were listening to something inside his belly. Suddenly he clapped his
hands; the singing stopped abruptly. In the silence he
shouted something which the "interpreter," Jack Steel, repeated. And before Jack Steel was through, Blind Hall was
shouting again, which the interpreter also repeated, and so
on, five or six times. It was not an exchange between Blind
Hall and Jack Steel. Jack Steel was simply repeating word
for word what Blind Hall was shouting. It was an exchange
between Hall and his poison, Raven. First, Hall would
shout a query which the interpreter repeated; then Hall
would listen to what Raven (hovering unseen above our
heads) was answering—and he would repeat that answer of
Raven which he, Hall, had heard in his mind—and the
interpreter would repeat the repetition. Then Hall emitted
a sort of grunted "Aaaah . . ." and relapsed into a brown
study. Everybody else, Jack Steel included, relaxed. Some
lit cigarettes; others gossiped. A woman said to me: "You

did pretty good; you help; that's good!" Robert Spring said: "Sure, everybody must help. Sometimes the poisons are far away. They don't hear. Everybody must sing together to wake them up."

BOOK OF THE HOPI

Frank Waters

Drawings and source materials recorded by
Oswald White Bear Fredericks

Unquestionably the best book ever published about the history, mythology and rituals of the Hopi Indians of the American Southwest. To Frank Waters the thirty-two Hopi elders told for the first time their legends, the meaning of their religious rituals and annual ceremonies, and their deeply rooted view of the world. The result is a beautiful and moving book, an important landmark in anthropology which brings to life again an Indian tribal culture now almost completely destroyed.

A LOOK AT SOCIETY
from
⒝⒝
BALLANTINE BOOKS

Indian Studies:

☐ **MASKED GODS** Frank Waters **24838** $1.95

☐ **"I WILL FIGHT NO MORE FOREVER"**
Merrill D. Beal **24840** $1.95

☐ **INDIAN ORATORY**
W. C. Vanderwerth **24890** $1.65

Anthropology and Archeology:

☐ **THE MOUND BUILDERS**
Robert Silverberg **24846** $1.50

☐ **THE BOG PEOPLE** P. V. Glob **24889** $1.65

☐ **THE TWILIGHT OF THE PRIMITIVE**
Lewis Cotlow **24895** $1.65

Communications:

☐ **I CAN SELL YOU ANYTHING**
Carl P. Wrighter **24844** $1.75

▼ Available at your local bookstore or mail the coupon below ▼

"This is one of the most beautiful books I have ever read, inside and out."

—Robert Kirsch
Los Angeles Times

SEVEN ARROWS

Hyemeyohsts Storm

A unique and moving novel about the ways of the Plains People by a Northern Cheyenne.

Superbly illustrated—over 150 pictures of faces and places, birds and animals of the Plains—and eight-tone color plates of the 13 symbolic shields, designed by Hyemeyohsts Storm and painted by Karen Harris.

25178/$7.95

To order by mail, send $7.95 per copy plus 50¢ per order for handling to Ballantine Cash Sales, P.O. Box 505, Westminster, Maryland 21157. Please allow three weeks for delivery.